DAFT AND DEADLY

The (Sort of) Beginning

MAPLE'S FANTASTIC STORIES

Book One

By the Mighty and
Awesome Maple Twiggs

ISBN: 978-1-952065-03-3

First edition.

Maple Twiggs Publishing.

For those who turn the light on for others, while they sit in the dark.

CONTENTS

CHAPTER ONE.

I Am Stella. Usually.

By Stella Grum.

April 27th.
Lunchtime.
The Wretched Courtyard of my Wretched High School.
Los Angeles.

Finn sat down next to me.

Goosebumps erupted across my forearms in a super obvious way.

Panicked, I quickly dumped the contents of my lunch bag onto the picnic table.

Why would he sit here? I had never talked to him before.

"Uh, you have really big eyes," he said to me.

What was this??

"You have really big teeth," I replied.

He winced and started to unwrap his sandwich.

"*Savage*," Julio whispered from across the table.

Um. I guess I'd missed the mark on that response.

Why was Finn talking to me though?

I looked to my left. Mikaela. That's who he really wanted to be sitting next to, chatting her up about eyeball dimensions.

I had learned this harsh lesson in kindergarten. If a hot guy talked to me it was because he wanted to get close to my attractive friend. He was too scared to just chat up the hot girl directly—so he used me as a far-less-intimidating starting target, a stepping-stone to his actual goal.

I was a wing-woman who had never signed up to be one. Which was painful.

I wonder if guys ever realize that we know what they're doing? Do they just not care if they hurt our feelings?

And now I get to eat my lunch in front of him.

Sigh.

As I struggled to open my pudding cup, my thumb swiftly punctured the foil lid and sunk into the pale rice goo.

I'm so classy.

I finished clawing the lid open and managed to shove a spoonful of pudding into my face.

I glanced again at Mikaela.

She had broken up with Matt a couple months ago. Matt had moved on to Chelsea before they had even broken up. (There are no secrets in high school.)

She glanced back at me, but her eyes were really searching for Finn.

Sigh.

I hung my pudding cup from my mouth and shoved the rest of my lunch back into the bag, as I clumsily got up from the color guard table.

As I walked away, out of the corner of my eye I saw Finn move over and start talking to Mikaela.

Probably about big eyes.

Yet another accomplishment in my tragic life-long career as an unintentional matchmaker.

Will there ever be a guy who sits down to talk with me because he actually wants to talk with *me*?

(Maple, the Marvelous Author of this Magnificent Tale: Mebbe.

Stella, the Unfortunate Protagonist of this Tale: Wait, does 'mebbe' mean yes or no?

Maple: Well, there *is* this guy in your future. He probably counts as someone who wants to talk with you.

Stella: What's his name? Is he cute? What does he look like? Where do I meet him? Does he know I'm weird and plain? Does he like me even though I'm weird and plain? And why is the author talking to me?

Maple: Slow down there. One thought at a time. The guy is cute. Very cute. I guess I can say that much. And his name's Archie. Oh and he's probably even more weird than you. Also, I'm talking with you because it's my book and I can do whatever I want.

Stella: Uh, okay. But. Archie? Archie. Archie? Hmmm. Isn't that like an old timey guy name from the 1940s? No one is named Archie today. That's a weird name for someone my age.

Maple: I didn't say he was your age.

Stella: Uhhhhhhhh. What??

Maple: Go back to eating. If you starve yourself you might kill your last brain cell.)

I crossed the courtyard, awkwardly holding my lunch.

No, I'm not in the color guard.

I don't have the required coordination or stamina.

Julio is my lab partner in Chemistry. But we don't have a deep, emotional bond. We just take turns saying "hand me that glass thingie" to each other.

I usually eat lunch by myself on the sunny concrete wall. But today it was too hot, so I was seeking shade—here in the wretched courtyard of my wretched high school of my wretched existence.

Clearly the color guard table was not going to be that refuge.

I eyeballed the art kids table, which was also in the shade. Henrietta was there. A girl who I sat next to in English.

She could draw like I wanted to.

"You're just tracing. You didn't actually draw it yourself, Stella," my father had told me when I proudly showed him my own rendition of a coloring book page when I was about ten.

I hadn't traced it. Not really. There was more than tracing there, I swear!

But still, there went my dreams of becoming an animator. Oh well.

So Henrietta is dating Jake. They are dating. Something like that. Which is fine.

I'm a bit bitter about that though.

At the beginning of the school year Jake displayed the same average appearance and heightened level of awkwardness as I did. Head down. Unkempt hair. Dark clothes. Hunched shoulders. Lack of eye contact.

'He must be my *destiny*'—I had thought, excitedly.

And stupidly.

Then he met Henrietta. Within an afternoon they were a couple. How does that even happen somewhere in the hallways between World History and Geometry???

Now he was smiling and laughing at the art kids table. This bugged me. I couldn't say I was 'jealous.' But more like shocked at the reversal. If someone like that can become how he is now, why can't I?

Should I try to steal him back?

Back from what, Stella? He was never yours in the first place, you idiot. And what makes you think he'll be as happy with you as he is with Henrietta?

Hearty guffaws erupted from the arty group.

I passed them by and kept walking.

(Stella: So, uh, Maple?

Maple: What?

Stella: What's up with this Archie guy? I need details.

Maple: What kinda details?

Stella: Like, what's gonna happen between him and me???

Maple: Well, you two are *sort of* destined to fall in love.

Stella: We are??? Uh. Uhhhhh. *Uhhhh?????
Really???*

Maple: But if you don't go back into this court-yard part of the story I'll never let you meet him, you turd.

Stella: But....)

Okay, let's look for shade.

Shade. Chorus table. Cassie from gym class. She was my possible in. She was bffs with the girl who could sing like I wanted to—Rebecca.

"You're just trying to repeat the sounds, but you're tone deaf," my father had explained to me as I finished my attempt to sound like Belle, that skinny peasant who belts out verses like a pro while dancing with sheep.

Clearly my showbiz life on Broadway was not going to happen. So much for that idea. I guess I didn't even have enough talent to be one of those lounge singers in slinky gowns who drape themselves across piano tops.

Sigh.

Cassie noticed me wandering about and waved me over to her table. A sign of an actual humane person.

But when I sat down, I was reminded as to why I preferred my too-sunny concrete wall.

"I think it's archery in gym today," she said.

"Yeah, I heard that, too," I replied.

And that was it. That was the whole conversation.

My solitary life with my widowed father had not taught me how to have a conversation in a group setting.

So I sat there. Chewing. And listening to everyone else talk about concerts.

Oranges, for some reason.

Then cars.

Movies.

And each other.

They all knew each other so well.

And I knew nothing.

(Stella: Maple, I've been thinking. I shouldn't

be this story's protagonist and half of a romantic couple. I don't have the self-esteem for that kind of gig.

Maple: I didn't ask for your opinion.

Stella: It's just—I don't think I'm ready to really fall in love with someone. I can't handle that kind of pressure.

Maple: I never suggested you could actually handle it.

Stella: Well, then why am I the main character if I'm going to freak out?

Maple: Stop trying to change my story and go to Algebra, you idiot.)

That afternoon in Algebra I non-purposefully eavesdropped on people's conversations as I doodled dark spirals in my notebook.

"Yeah, Jessie's older brother died this weekend in a motorcycle accident. That's why she's not in school today," one girl said to her friend.

I looked up and across the room at the empty chair.

Thank goodness Jessie wasn't in school today. Phew. Dodged that catastrophe.

I had never had a single conversation with her, but if she *were* in school—well, aren't you sup-

posed to say something to someone who is griev-
ing?

But I wouldn't have a clue what to say to her.

'It sucks that your brother died.'

Would that be enough?

Doesn't seem like it.

"So April 26th is her Dad's birthday. But her
brother died on the way to the party. Can you imagine? Now it's like that day is ruined forever," the
girl continued.

I tried to think of these two girls' names.

I wouldn't have even known Jessie's name if they
hadn't said it out loud.

I guess I'm senile.

The image of my mother's picture in our living
room flashed into my mind. I *am* senile. I don't
even remember the date of *her* death.

(Does that make me a bad daughter???)

Although, I can't remember the first six years of
my life, so I guess that's not surprising.

But wait, has my Dad even told me which day
she died?

I don't think he has.

That's weird right?

(Maple: Yes. That *is* weird. It's really weird *and*

suspicious. It's almost as if he's hiding something from you. And it's *also* really weird and suspicious that you can't remember the first six years of your life. You freak.

Stella: Um. If he's hiding something from me *AND* you're the author, then you'd know what he's hiding. So you can just tell me. Since you're here now. Again.

Maple: Oh. Uh.

Stella: *And* you can tell me why I can't remember the first six years of my life. Since you can't seem to shut up.

Maple: I can't explain all that stuff to you yet because I'm still working on it. Stay tuned.

Stella: What the?)

I glanced at Jessie's two friends.

Their conversation had continued in a normal fashion while I was arguing with the author in my head. Or in her head.

"I'm gonna move out of my Aunt's house next week," Girl One said as she anxiously tapped her pen against the desk. "All we do is fight. And my Grandma agreed that I should go live at my Dad's house instead."

"So your Dad's okay with that?"

"Yeah, he and my uncles are gonna help me move, too."

Huh. High school freshmen can just pick up and change houses? Is that a thing?

It's almost as if she made the decision herself.

Can high school freshmen make their own decisions?

I certainly don't feel like my Dad would let me make that kind of decision, or any kind of decision really.

But why would I move out?

Do *I* fight with my Dad a lot?

Hmmm. I don't think so.

But there is this constant odd tension.

Like he'll blow up in anger at any moment.

And sometimes he does.

Does that count as fighting?

Well, even if that does count as fighting, I'd have no place to go. What's it like to have another house to move to?

What's it like to have a grandmother who agrees with your plans? What's it like to have grandparents?

I looked up as the Algebra teacher entered the room.

"Blah, blah, blah, blah, bah, bah, bah, baaaaaa,"

he said as he started drawing math stuff on the board.

I'm sure those were real words, but I couldn't keep track of them so don't expect me to write them here.

I could pretend that I spent the next hour listening to him, but instead I was thinking about Jason.

'Who is Jason???'—I hear you ask.

Well, he's the senior who lives across the street and mows his lawn once a week.

Who plants grass in Southern California??? I mean, the audacity. Everyone else just has rocks, dry scrubby bushes and cacti like us. But no, Jason's parents had to have a lawn.

And thank goodness.

Every week on lawn day I rush home from school, grab my box of cereal and an iced tea, and sit in my living room bay window.

Then I watch Jason push his mower back and forth.

In his light gray jersey pants. That move like silk against...wait, I can't describe this part to you.

It's embarrassing.

Never mind.

Let's skip ahead.

I wonder if this Archie person wears light gray

jersey pants....

"Whatcha doin'?" my father asked as I coughed dry cereal bits across the bay window seat in shock.

He was home early.

And he had caught me watching Jason.

Uh.

But neither one of us wanted to say out loud what I had been doing.

Even though we both knew what I had been doing.

Until he snuck up and scared the poop out of me.

He totally did that on purpose, didn't he?

"So Mr. Banerat called me today, and I don't think you're going to have TV privileges until you get your Algebra grade up."

I went back to staring out the window at Jason. Sweet, comforting Jason.

He doesn't '*think*' I'm going to have TV privileges? Is he punishing me or negotiating with me? Why does he have to be so annoying?

All.

The.

Time.

Sigh.

(p.s. I never did get those TV privileges back.)

"I lied to you," I said to him the next morning while we ate breakfast.

But I had no clue why.

I looked up from my bowl of cereal, meeting his gaze.

"About what?" he asked.

"About the plastic container I wanted to give to the President of the Ernest Hemingway Fan Club," I said.

Confusion spread across both our faces.

Then the pain was sudden and crippling. Like someone had just shot an arrow through my skull.

My eyes watered and I collapsed off the chair onto the floor, holding my head.

And then my nose started to bleed.

Everywhere.

It was gross.

My father got up and fled the room.

Probably the best tactic.

He returned with a washcloth for me to hold against my cursed nostrils.

Then he went to the kitchen cabinets and got a dishpan to catch all of the blood the washcloth wasn't able to absorb.

And then he left the room again, I assume to call 911.

But an ambulance never arrived.

Instead he came back with more washcloths.

And eventually he retrieved a cold washcloth that he put across my forehead when the blood stopped flowing.

"I think this must be a migraine," I whispered.

He left and came back with some pills and water.

Which I choked down.

I curled up into the fetal position on the floor, covered in my own nose-blood, eyes tightly shut, head splitting with pain.

So this is what death feels like.

"I'll call the school and the doctor's office," he said.

And then he left me there.

Never asked me what I had lied to him about.

Never asked who the President of the Ernest Hemingway Fan Club was.

Shouldn't he be inquiring further about those things?

Not that I had a clue how to answer him.

I have no idea why I even said those things.

Isn't this the point where he yells at me for not

taking care of myself well enough to prevent this kind of nosebleed and migraine?

'Why do you always get sick?!'—should have come out of his mouth by now.

"Message your friends to get class notes for you today!" my father announced from the living room.

Oh, yes.

Friends.

If I had those I would be sure to do that.

I pressed the washcloth onto my forehead with one hand, hoping that it would somehow sink into my skull and take this pain away.

I thought back to yesterday in the courtyard.

I held my other hand in front of my eyes, and started to count the friends I could message for class notes on my fingers.

None of the fingers moved.

CHAPTER TWO.

To Morrow.

By Morrow Demington.

(Morrow: Maple! Ugh. 'To Morrow.' Really??? Don't do that. Don't ever write 'To Morrow' ever again when introducing me.

Maple: *sticks out tongue*

Morrow: Sigh.)

April 28th.

(Yeah, that date should look sort of familiar.)

Some Early Morning Hour Before Anyone is Really Awake.

The Road in Front of Our House.

Badger's Wood.

The Middle of Nowhere, i.e. Northern Connecticut.

"It's a black sedan!!!" Nora screamed as she darted out of the road and dramatically rolled into the ditch, purposefully slamming her back into our fence.

Her twin sister Ellie squealed and ran in the opposite direction, accidentally tripping on her way across the street.

"Here comes a red convertible!!!" I yelled, as I threw myself on top of Ellie.

"You know, just because you're younger than me doesn't mean you're smaller!" Ellie said, groaning, as she pushed my faux corpse off of herself.

I wasn't really dead.

And there weren't really any cars forcing us off the road.

There was no sedan. No convertible. No other vehicle.

Ever.

This was a game we played. Invisible Cars.

Yes. It *is* as pathetic as it sounds.

We stand in the road outside of our house and dodge pretend cars.

Yes.

That's one of the many ways we entertain ourselves, depressingly, here in the middle of nowhere, where no one ever drives by. And I mean never, ever. In my entire life I've never seen anyone come here.

I wonder if I could magically *create* cars that could run us over?

I mean, not run me over.

Just my sisters.

I wonder if our magical powers can do that?

Hmmm. I should take this opportunity to start a 'real' conversation with my 'lovely' sisters.

"So about this morning…" I began.

"Oh, *that*," Nora said.

Then she started giggling as she casually rolled around in the dirt like a puppy.

Yes, I had tried to ask our adult overlord—Penny —a question this morning as we ate breakfast.

And yes, I had failed at it.

"What exactly is the House of Coventry?" I asked her.

I knew we had lived there once upon a time before being trapped in these woods like hermits. And I wanted to know more.

"What do you want to know?" Penny asked.

Answering a question with a question.

I hate that.

It was her normal evasive technique.

"Everything," I answered.

There take that, you red-haired poop!

She immediately started coughing as a well-timed distraction.

"There's no point in avoiding this," Eagle said, glaring at Penny, and then he cleared his throat as if to give a speech.

She poked him in his fuzzy rabbit tummy and then got up from the table to wash dishes and wipe down the counters and not be anywhere near me, the girl asking horrible questions.

So that didn't go anywhere.

But now we were outside and away from Penny.

Maybe someone would tell me something.

"So what is the House of Coventry, really?" I asked.

Ellie grabbed a twig that was next to her knee and began to draw three numbered columns in the dirt.

"The House of Coventry refers to more than one thing," she explained. "First, it's the common parlance for the Realm of Destruction, owned by the God of Destruction—Suntsitzea."

"What's he like?" I asked.

"I know he's gone missing," Nora said. "I heard Eagle say that once. And no one can find him."

"I hadn't heard that. And I haven't read anything

specific about him yet in my studies," Ellie added, looking frustrated. "There's got to be a book out there all about him though, right?"

Nora and I looked at each other and shrugged.

What would we know about what exists beyond this house and these woods?

"Well, anyway. Where was I? Okay. Second, the House of Coventry is also the lejerdemani family that served Suntsitzea, and helped maintain his Realm. Essentially the Realm's dynastic nobility," Ellie continued.

"Like kings and queens?" I asked.

"No. More like dukes and duchesses. Suntsitzea is the sort of king," Ellie said. "Or was the king. Wherever he is."

"Did he wear a crown and puffy velvet shorts with tights???" Nora asked.

"How would I know? But I don't think so. And also, stop being weird," Ellie said. "Third, it's the main residence of the Coventry family, located in the Realm of Destruction, and comprised of the destroyed Gilded Age mansions that lined Central Park in old, skyscraper-free New York."

"So we three were born in the House of Coventry—the Realm, the family, and the specific building?" I asked.

"Yes," Ellie said.

I suddenly felt like she was actually way more intelligent than she had ever let on. Hadn't she just been reading fashion magazines and buffing her nails for the last half a dozen years???

"So how can we go there?" Nora asked.

"We can't," Ellie replied. "Don't be stupid. Penny would never let us leave the cottage and these woods."

"Well, but, what's it like there?" I asked. "Do you know, Ellie?"

"Hmmm. The House is as old as time," she said. "As old as human creativity. Everything that was destroyed here on Earth went there, to the Realm of Destruction. Ghosts are allowed to come and go freely. So they can inhabit their old childhood home that was torn down, or tour glorious mansions destroyed during revolutions, or walk the streets of lost cities. Everything that was ever destroyed exists there simultaneously, overlapping, and yet also separate, like the pages of a big book that you can flip through and see history unfold. You know, you'd already know about all of this if you just read the right history books."

How was she already reading history books?

She must be joking.

We were just reading about mice and cookies the other day.

"*Which* books have *you* been reading?!" Eagle asked her, appearing out of thin air, his eyes wide.

"The books you gave me," she said.

"Oh yeah. Maybe I shouldn't have done that. Although, I shouldn't have done a lot of things. That's the least of them."

"So why don't I remember anything about this place?" I asked.

"Because you're a moron. Same goes for your sisters here," Eagle replied.

"I object, your Honor," Nora said. "I prefer the term logic-challenged!"

"And why doesn't Penny want to talk about it? Like at all? Ever?" I pushed.

"It's a sensitive topic. Like foot fungus," Eagle said.

I glared at him in response.

"Well, the past wasn't a walk in the park. Penny was your mother's best friend, and ten years ago she rescued you all from the House when you were just a baby," he said to me. "Let's just say that was the end of a chain of failed missions. And because it was just one heaping pile of steaming failure on top of another, we've never returned to that place."

"If we had stayed there we probably would've been killed. Just like our parents, and our grandparents, and our great-grandparents. And many other family members," Ellie added.

We all took turns looking at each other in silence.

But I wasn't going to let this end here.

I wanted more information, dang it!!

"Uh. Does that mean it's a dangerous place?" I asked.

"It is now. But once upon a time, it was your home," Eagle said. "Maybe it was always a dangerous place, and we just didn't know that. When Suntsitzea disappeared, your great-grandfather tried to manage it all on his own, but even a Coventry lejerdemani can't handle that kind of responsibility. And it just sort of dissolved into a mad chaos."

And my great-grandfather couldn't stop the traumatic events that led to his death, and my sisters and me being orphaned.

Which is why this is such an awkward topic to discuss.

Could anyone have prevented what happened?

I wonder.

I looked over at Nora. She was now drawing rude images into the dirt with her finger. Ellie was staring at the bark of a tree as if her life depended on it.

I guess they don't remember much about all of this either.

Or they don't want to.

"Luckily *you are all morons*, so even if you can remember that place, you're probably too stupid to know what your memories mean," Eagle continued.

I scowled at him.

Gosh. Harsh much?

Sure my sisters were dumb.

But I wasn't dumb.

I'm the smartest one in this whole book.

"You know, I really wanted a description of the House of Coventry like the start of that famous ring book," Nora interrupted. "It rhymes, and has a ton of mystic, mysterious stuff. Numbers and rings. Elves. Dwarves. Stone halls. Doomed men. Thrones. Dark ones. Shadows over lands. Repetition of key elements in a poetic manner. One ring. One ring. Yadda yadda. And stuff binding in the darkness. I mean, who doesn't want to be bound in the darkness, amiright? Can one of you make that explanation more poetic, and rhymeee-ish and like a magical, mystery tour?"

"No," Eagle said. "Stop being so logic-challenged."

"But I have needs. I need a fancy elf poem!"

"No," Ellie said. "We don't have narrative space to repeat all of that in a new way."

"You're a butthole."

"You're a bigger butthole."

"You're the biggest butthole."

Uh.

How was I ever going to learn anything from this bunch of clowns???

"Hold on, hold on," I interjected, trying to steer the conversation away from buttholes and back to the real topic. "If you guys know everything—why, if we're just lejerdemani, why are *we* so different?"

Surely this question would stump them. We could practice magic since we were about five, and that just wasn't normal for a lejerdemani. So, why?

"We're only part lejerdemani, but also part something else. It's a mystery," Nora answered.

How did she know that?

"Or at least, no one has yet to explain *to us* what our father was," Ellie said.

And then she glared at Eagle.

"Penny's not going to tell us," Nora said. "But I know he wasn't human, and he wasn't a lejerde-mani. That's all I got out of her so far."

And then she glared at Eagle.

"Does that make him a god?" I asked.

"I'm not sure," Ellie replied, while still glaring at Eagle.

So I also started glaring at Eagle, who disappeared into thin air.

"Clearly that furbuttball isn't going to answer that question either," Ellie complained.

"Do you think our Dad was a *vampire*???" Nora asked.

"How'd you get to be so dumb?" I asked her. "Really? No. There aren't vampires in this book."

Nora stuck her tongue out at me.

"We must be weird magical mutts whose powers manifested early. Much earlier than they should have," Ellie said, shrugging.

"However, we aren't *actually* allowed to use our abilities," I said quietly.

"Penny forbids it for our protection," Ellie said. "You know that."

Yes, I knew that. Duh.

But I'd been trying to find a way around that, unbeknownst to my sisters.

You readers should probably know that when Penny rescued us she took us to her grandfather's cottage, deep in the woods. Far from any signs of humanity. And then she formed a magical protective bubble around the cottage and part of the wood so that no one would be able to find us.

Nora: I named the bubble Sven, by the way.

Um. No one cares, you weirdo.

Where was I? Oh yeah—so why the need for a bubble?

Someone, or something, had been hunting down lejerdemani and killing them.

This included 99.9% of our family.

My sisters and I were all that was left of our bloodline.

Whoever the murderer, or murderers, were—they had an amazing ability to track the lejerdemani, no matter where they were.

And that's why we had the bubble.

Penny's grandfather had spent years developing the magic to make such a force field. And she employed it to protect us. But if we, the freakish Demington sisters, started practicing magic inside of the bubble, it might be compromised and we might find the enemy at our doorstep.

Which is why Penny forbids us from practicing magic.

And even from learning about it.

Which, I thought, was slightly unfair.

We should *at least* be able to learn about it.

Which is why I had been poking around in all of the nooks and crannies of the old cottage, looking for books, papers, notes—anything, really—that Penny's grandfather had left behind that might teach me about magic.

Penny had locked up his study, so that was a no-go.

It's not like my moral code kept me from trying to pick the lock on that door.

I had certainly tried, dozens of times.

But I eventually figured out that she had enchanted the door so that only she could unlock it. So breaking in wasn't going to work for me. (At least not until I learned about magic myself.)

So after failing to find any shred of educational material on magic in the house, I tried outside in the garden.

(Nora: Which is where I come in.
Ellie: I think it was my idea to go into the woods.
Nora: Um, no. It was totally mine.

30

Morrow: It doesn't really matter whose idea it was.

Nora: You wouldn't say that if you were the one who had the idea. No, no. Let's lay out this story and see whose idea it was.

Morrow: Fine. Let's do that, you nutballs.)

After that semi-productive conversation in the road, I decided to look in Penny's grandfather's greenhouse for any information on magic.

Penny was diligently cleaning something. Maybe the laundry. I didn't really care what. Eagle was harassing her, per usual, while pretending to help. My sisters were reading in the library.

I had a small window of time to carry out my activities undetected. Or so I thought.

"What are you doing *in here*?" Nora asked as she burst through the greenhouse doors, attempting to surprise me. (I only peed myself a little.)

"Nothing."

"You're lying."

"Maybe. What are you gonna do about it?"

"Hmmmm. Maybe I'll tell Ellie where you are and she can tell you all about this book she's been reading on clothing styles of the 1960s. And then she can bore you to death as well."

"Is that why you came outside? To avoid her?"

"Maybe. But anyway, don't try to distract me from my question! What are you doing in here?"

It had already been a month of me playing kid detective around the house. It was inevitable that my sisters would start to wonder what I was doing. I stood there pondering whether or not I should tell Nora what I was trying to accomplish. She stood there making funny faces at me, trying to get me to crack.

Then Ellie showed up.

"Norad, I was just getting into the chapter on 1960s hairstyles, where'd you go? Why'd you come out here?"

(Norad is Nora's nickname. Look it up. It pretty much sums up her nosey, destructive personality.)

I sighed heavily.

Now it was back to the three amigos.

My quiet, alone time had been even briefer than usual today.

This is what happens when you don't have to go to school. (And because Penny limits our TV and Internet time—she thinks they melt your brain cells.) You end up spending way, *way* too much quality bonding time with your siblings.

It's horrible.

"Well?" Nora asked me. "Do you want to tell us what you're doing in here, or do you want to learn about the birth of the beehive from Ellie?"

I winced in mental anguish. The second option was not an option, in my mind.

"The truth is, I'm looking for information on practicing magic," I answered.

"You're what?" Nora asked.

"You heard me. I want to learn about magic. And everything is locked away in Horace's study. But there must be something else in this house, right? I mean, it's been the home of a lejerdemani family for generations."

"Why would Horace leave anything in his greenhouse?" Nora asked.

"Well, I've looked all through the house without any luck, so I thought I'd try out here."

"*Practicing* magic, huh?" Ellie asked. "I've never read anything about that, even from the books Eagle gave me. What about the woods?"

"Why would there be information on magic in the woods?" I asked.

"The ruins of a cottage are out there. I found them once. It was either knocked down or burnt down. I'm not sure which," Ellie explained.

"And the ruins are inside Sven?" Nora asked.

We couldn't leave the bubble.

Yes—that's right—we hadn't left this house and wood since I was about 5 months old.

Can you say: 'sheltered existence?'

"They're just at the edge of it," Ellie replied. "How could I have found them if they were outside the bubble? You idjit."

"That's digit, isn't it Ellie?" I asked. "You mean digit."

"No, idjit means a stupid person," she said. "Sort of like a person who doesn't know about the word...idjit."

(Morrow: Okay, hold on here, author person? Maple? You're making me out to be an idjit on purpose aren't you?

Maple: Maybe.

Morrow: *Whhhyyyyy???*

Maple: You said you're the smartest one in this novel.

Morrow: So?

Maple: So you are now being punished for your presumptuousness.

Morrow: I hate you.

Maple: I know. *makes kissy face*)

"So what should we do?" I asked.

"We should go to the ruins," Nora said.

"What? No. All three of us together? That will look suspicious," I said.

"What do you mean? The three of us are always together. What's suspicious about that? You want to see the ruins. I want to see them. And Ellie knows where they are. So we all have to be there."

"Eagle's totally gonna figure out what we're doing and track us down in the woods and scare the poop out of us. I just know it," I said.

"What's new?" Nora responded.

"True. True," I said and sighed.

"Um, I'll show you guys where they are. But if Eagle finds us, this wasn't my idea," Ellie said.

So we tromped through the woods like those kids in that disturbing finding-a-corpse movie, but without the railroad tracks to follow.

"Do you think there are any dead bodies at the ruins?" Nora asked, apparently reading my mind about the corpse movie thing.

"What? *What*? No. Are there? Could there be? Morrow, is she right? Will there be dead bodies?" Ellie asked, panicking.

"Ellie, you're the one who's been there before. Did you see any dead bodies?" I asked.

"No."

"So, there you go. No dead bodies. Calm down."

"There could be skeletons though," Nora whispered.

"*What?!?*" Ellie asked.

"Do you guys really think Penny and Eagle would be okay with us living next to a ruin with skeletons in it?" I asked.

"People live next to cemeteries all the time," Nora explained.

"You aren't helping," I told her.

"I know. And it's fantastic."

Ellie started walking slower, her eyes darting around the woods, looking carefully where she was stepping.

"It's fine, Ellie. There aren't going to be any dead bodies or skeletons at this place. You would've found them last time."

"But I wasn't looking for them! They could've been right there!"

"Let's just walk there in silence, can we do that?" I asked.

"No. That's not possible," Nora said.

"Well, it's just a bit further, but you guys have to check it out first before I'll get close to it," Ellie whined.

We reached what I had thought was the edge of the bubble—the edge of a plateau that fell away down a steep escarpment, which dipped down into a deeply wooded area. But Ellie kept walking down the slope. More like sliding really, down the leaf-strewn hillside, avoiding trees and branches on her way down.

"How did you figure out to go down the hill?" I asked. "I thought the end of the bubble was up there?"

"I thought so too, until...."

"Until you fell down the hill and ended up at the bottom of it," Nora said.

"How did you know that?" Ellie asked, astounded at her sister's psychic abilities.

"Just a guess."

Ellie was certainly the least-coordinated Demington.

It was a rough descent, but we eventually made it to the base of the hill. Where we found the ruins of the cottage, well-hidden behind a line of thick oak trees and under over-grown, but dead, shrubs and vines.

"How long do you think it's been like this?" Nora asked.

"Who knows. But it couldn't be too long. These

vines aren't over everything yet," I answered.

The foundation of a fairly large cottage was still visible, but only bricks and stones remained. There were no wooden walls or roof left. Some timbers lay here and there, but it was like a storm had passed through and blown away most of what would have been a house's rubble.

There wasn't a basement, just a ground floor with a large colonial-style fireplace—which was really the only thing still standing besides a few chunks of the kitchen walls. It was the kind of fireplace that you could almost walk right into and it took up one whole wall of the kitchen.

Nora went over to the fireplace-wall-thingy and started ripping all of the vines and weeds from it.

"*What are you doing?!?*" Ellie asked, shocked.

"Looking for dead bodies!" Nora said, with wide eyes and a mocking tone.

"What *are* you doing?" I asked in a more skeptical manner.

"Well, you wanted to find stuff about magic, right? How can we look at anything here if it's under all these plants?" she asked.

True enough.

"Plus, I think this fireplace has some symbols on the bricks in the back of it. I can see little shapes," she added.

"You can?" I asked.

Now I was interested. A pile of bricks covered in dead weeds was not exciting. Symbols on an old, abandoned fireplace? Now that's more my speed. I started helping her tear off the vines.

"I'll help you guys, but make sure there aren't any dead things over there first," Ellie chimed in.

"Just the squirrel corpse next to your foot," Nora said.

Ellie screamed and almost passed out.

"There's no dead squirrel!" I quickly interjected. "There's no need to make extra noise and draw Eagle out here, guys. Remember? So cut it out, Nora."

"Pppttsssshhh," was her highly educated response.

The three of us spent the next half an hour ripping most of the plants off of the fireplace. Some alive, most dead.

My hands stung when the work was done. But my mind was satisfied. There were indeed symbols on the bricks of this fireplace. 24 symbols. Each on its own brick.

Unfortunately, I had no idea what they meant.

"A flame. A crane. A stone," I said. "What could

these possibly mean?"

"It must be some sort of code," Nora said. "Two dogs snarling at each other. A heart. A dove. Clearly it means something. But I have no clue."

"They're iconic attributes," Ellie said. "Look. The sieve here and the flame would be for Scrupulousness. He is usually an old man holding a sieve in front of a fiery furnace, which tests metals. He uses the sieve to separate good actions from bad actions."

"A fiery furnace? Tests metals? Scrupulousness?" Nora asked. "What language are you speaking???"

"You know, icons. Emblems. Pictorial representations of vices, virtues, the elements, the arts, celestial bodies, etc. Don't you guys read? Like Justice with her blindfold and scales—she's an icon and those are her attributes."

"But what does scrupulousness even mean?" Nora asked, laughing at the weirdness of the word.

"Carefulness. Conscientiousness. A person with scruples is hesitant to do anything they believe is wrong," Ellie explained. "For example, a person with scruples wouldn't borrow her sister's hairdryer without asking, break it, and then put it back without admitting that she broke it."

"I still can't figure out how you found out I did

that," Nora whined.

"Eagle told me."

"That darn rabbit."

"But anyway," I jumped in before the whole conversation was derailed into an argument about a hairdryer. "You're saying all of these symbols are attributes of icons, like Scrupulousness (I admit I did have a difficult time pronouncing that word right then) and Justice?"

"Yes," Ellie answered.

"But why would they be at the back of a fireplace?" I asked.

"If this were my cottage, I'd have a secret passageway or portal. Maybe they're for that," Nora suggested.

"I think you read too much fiction," I responded.

"Well, they're most likely there for some sort of code at least. I mean, why else would anyone use these symbols? They could've just made bricks with pretty flowers on them," Ellie added.

"Good point. But what are we supposed to do with them? Read them in some way? Like they're a message?" I wondered.

"They open a secret passageway. I just know it," Nora said.

"And what would a secret passageway from a

ruined fireplace in the middle of nowhere lead to exactly, Miss Genius?" I asked her.

"Well, it might lead out of this bubble—for one thing," Ellie replied.

And we all looked at each other with wide eyes.

"We can't do that," Nora whispered. "We can't leave Sven."

"We're not *supposed* to leave the bubble, Norad. 'Can't' and 'not supposed to' are two different things," Ellie said.

"Before we get ahead of ourselves, we should examine these images more closely," I said.

I started to gently brush the dirt off the bricks.

Nora nearly pushed me aside and started trying to push them in—as if one of them would pop in like a button and a hidden door would just swing open.

"Tiger. Hourglass. Rooster. Sun. Pair of wings. Sword. Helmet. Pillar. Maybe you just have to touch them all in a specific order?" Nora asked, out loud, to no one in particular.

Because it's not like Ellie or I knew the answer to her question.

I rolled my eyes.

"It's not gonna work. Pushing against them is probably just gonna knock down the ruins of the fireplace, you moron," I said.

"An axe-spear thingy. An oak branch. A sheep," she continued pushing and pushing anyway, ignoring me, per usual. "A ring. A—wait, the ring moved."

"Huh?" I asked. "What do you mean?"

"It vibrated underneath my hand when I pushed against it."

"No way," I replied.

But then I tried it myself, and the brick did vibrate, just slightly.

"What was the order you just pushed those in?" Ellie asked.

"I don't remember!" Nora whined.

"No, no you said axe-spear thingy, oak branch, sheep, ring," I answered.

So we pushed those again, in that order. Just the vibration of the ring happened. Nothing else vibrated and nothing else happened.

"Well, it's not like those four things are actually all attributes for an icon," Ellie said. "So what would they possibly do together?"

"You said all of these things are icon attributes," Nora said.

"Yeah. But those four things aren't attributes for the same icon. That's not just one icon," Ellie explained.

"So, wait. What if we are looking for the symbols that all connect to just one icon? Like the ring, and some other things. And if we push them in order, then something will happen?" I wondered.

"Which icon has a ring as an attribute, Ellie? And what are that icon's other attributes?" Nora pressured her.

"Okay, I'm smart. But I'm not that smart. We're gonna have to look it up. It's not like I have the whole 'Iconologia' memorized."

I sighed. Deeply.

I didn't even know what an 'Icono-something' was, never mind having it memorized. I had been so sure that I was hot stuff, sneaking around like a kid detective (mostly just disturbing dust bunnies instead of finding clues). And meanwhile my sister Ellie was secretly becoming a freaking encyclopedia. I honestly felt a little bitter, and like I had been wasting my time with my detective role-playing.

"What's an Icono..." I started.

"Logia," Ellie finished. "It's a book. It was in the library at home."

"Alright, let's go back and find information

about a ring attribute in this book. Then we'll come back here and figure this out together," I said as I tried to resign myself to the thought that Ellie was simply better at this type of investigation.

"Good thinking, Team Leader Mu!" Nora agreed.

"What are you calling me now?" I asked.

"Mu—from the Greek Alphabet. The word for 'M.' Like for 'N' it would be Nu, and for 'E' it would be Epsilon," she said. "At first I thought Ellie would be our Team Leader, since she does seem to be the smartest one here. And Team Leader Epsilon sounded pretty darn awesome. So I went with the Greek letter idea. But then you seem to be giving the orders, so that makes you more of the Team Leader. But unfortunately 'M' is Mu and that just doesn't sound as cool as Epsilon. Sorry about that."

"You're weird. Stop being weird," I replied.

"I don't want to be the Team Leader anyway," Ellie added. "They have to make too many decisions. I don't want that kind of responsibility."

And there she was. There was the sister I knew so well, and loved, some of the time. The delicate flower, always standing in the corner—filing her nails—watching everyone else do the dirty work.

I marked down all of the fireplace symbols in my

notebook, carried with me for the fruitless greenhouse search, and then we tromped back through the woods to our house's library.

Ellie pulled out Cesare Ripa's "Iconologia," the P. Tempest London edition of MDCCIX, from underneath a large bookshelf in the back of the library.

As I watched Ellie flip through the front of the book, I realized that its thick brown leather binding had helped it blend in with the wood floor. I never even knew it was there.

"How'd you even know this thing was here? I've never seen it before in my life. *I didn't know there were books on the floor under the cases???*" I said, very exasperated.

Apparently I *really* sucked at being a kid detective. I couldn't even find a secret book that my sister had discovered ages ago and had already read cover to cover.

"This was the only one on the floor," Ellie stated. "And I only found it because I dropped my nail file, and when I bent down to pick it up—there was a book sitting down there in the dark."

Ah. The nail file.

Yes.

Of course.

"MDCCIX means 1709," she continued as she

pointed to the title page.

"Thank you, Internet," Nora replied.

Ellie stuck out her tongue at her.

"Well, like I said—I only read it through once. I didn't memorize it," Ellie said. "Each of the icons is shown and then their attributes are listed across from the pictures in little paragraphs. But there isn't a glossary of symbols. You can't look up 'ring' and then find which icons use that as an attribute."

She—lectured. Yes, it felt like a lecture. Sigh. She was enjoying this.

"So what you're saying is that we have to read this whole thing in order to find out which icons use rings?" Nora whined.

"Yes, that's exactly what I'm saying. But it can't really be that many icons that have a ring as an attribute—I would think. I wish I could remember though…."

I already felt my brain going numb.

Mind you, I loved reading.

But I loved action much more. Actually doing something.

And when I did read, I preferred action: spies doing sneaky spy stuff, detectives hunting down criminals, Wild West shoot-outs, ninja assassins attacking emperors. This was annoying to sit down and search a whole darn book before we could actually do something with that fireplace.

"Not it!!!" my sisters called out simultaneously, as I sat there drifting off into my own thoughts, drooling on myself in pre-boredom.

Their pointer fingers were firmly planted on the sides of their respective noses.

And it suddenly became my job to skim this whole book for the word 'ring.'

"Uggghhhghghhhghgh," I burbled out in anguish. "How many of these icons are there???"

"326," Ellie answered.

My gawd.

"And just so you know, sometimes the 'esses' look like weird 'effs.' But other times they don't," she added.

"The what?"

"Like manifest, sometimes it looks like manifeft. It's the Old English style of making an 'ess' in a publication. They're long and thin and look like weird 'effs.'"

"Thanks. I needed something bizarre to complicate my search," I groaned.

So I spent the next who-knows-how-many hours reading through that book, prepared to take notes on every icon that used a ring as an attribute.

But it turned out there was only one.

"It's Secrecy," I told my sisters, who had both been pretending to read other books in the library while actually just staring at me until I found all the icons that used a ring. "Page 68, Fig. 271. '*Secretezza, overo Taciturnita*: A very grave Lady all in black, carrying a Ring to her Mouth, as if she intended to seal it up. Grave, because there is no greater Sign of Lightness than to divulge a Friend's Secrets. In Black denotes Constancy, never taking any other Colour. The Ring is the Emblem of Secrecy and Friendship.'"

"So wait, there's a grave? Like a tombstone?" Nora asked.

"No, I don't think one of the attributes is a grave. It says 'a very grave lady,' which means she has a very serious look about her. She takes knowing someone else's secrets very seriously," Ellie answered.

I admit—I had no idea what any part of that paragraph on Secrecy meant. But don't tell my sisters that. I mean, I know what the words meant individually. But strung together in that way, well— I was lost.

"So what exactly are Secrecy's attributes then?" Nora inquired.

"Well, there weren't any colored bricks, so I don't think 'black' counts. Instead I would think something like a pair of lips for the ring to seal up, as if it were a signet ring, used to seal papers by pressing it into melted wax. Like gluing an envelope shut to seal a letter," Ellie explained.

"Who would want to press hot wax onto their lips with a ring?" Nora pondered.

If you're thinking 'a masochist,' dear reader—well, yes. But we aren't writing that novel either.

"No one is pressing hot wax to their lips," Ellie said and sighed. "It's a metaphor. Anyway, Morrow, was there a brick with a pair of lips on it?"

I checked my notebook.

"Well, yes. There was. I thought it was kinda like a kiss though, so I wrote down 'kiss' instead of lips. My bad."

"Sealed with a kiss! SWAK. Except it's—sealed with a ring. SWAR? Does that work?" Nora thought out loud, like the crazy person she was.

"Focus, people," Ellie commanded. "I think we should go back and try to press the bricks with the lips and the ring at the same time. And see what happens."

So we hiked back through the woods to the cottage ruins.

"I feel like we should be riding our bikes through pine-tree-lined, winding roads in the rolling hills of the Northwest while listening to '80s pop," Nora announced.

"We aren't those Goo-kids," I responded. "I doubt we're going to find pirate treasure behind that fireplace."

"Well, at least one of us should be wearing a yellow rain slicker," Nora added.

I shook my head 'no.'

"A red sweatband?"

I shook my head 'no' again.

"A Hawaiian shirt with pink hibiscus on it? Or is that hibiscuses? Hibiscuseses? Hibisci? Hibiscus flowers. There that works."

"Don't make me slap you," I warned.

"Would you two shut up," Ellie whined. "We're almost there."

We were indeed almost there. And after we managed to tumble our way down the hill, and trip into the ruins—we stood in front of the fireplace staring at it. Like morons.

"You do it," Ellie told me.

"You do it," I returned.

"I'll do it!" Nora replied.

"Nooo!" Ellie and I said together, in panic.

"What's wrong?" Nora asked.

"Well, what if this is something big? What if this does open a door beyond the bubble? You know we aren't supposed to go outside the bubble," I answered.

"I'm mostly afraid of the unknown," Ellie added. "Anything could happen. Or nothing. Or anything. It's like London's Klondike. Unexplored. A metaphor for the undiscovered passages of the psyche that could either make or break a character. He always killed off characters that allowed themselves to be overcome by fear. Fear of the unknown. The unknowable. Of eternity."

"Is this the part with your mental breakdown?" I asked her.

"I'm saying—I'm saying, what if there are dead people or zombies or monsters connected to this fireplace?" she asked.

I stared at her blankly. Knowing that there were no words in existence that could really soothe a crazy person.

"*Or dead zombie monster Klondike wolf squirrels?!?!?*" Nora asked, in fake panic.

Ellie rolled her eyes.

"Ehhhhh," Nora continued. "You guys would stand and stare at this fireplace for the rest of your lives if you could. But what does that do? Nothing."

Nora stepped forward and pushed against the two bricks in question.

They slid inward, about an inch, and we heard a clicking sound.

A cool breeze whipped through the woods.

Then the whole wall of 24 bricks melted away before our eyes as if it had just been painted there.

And indeed, there was a secret entrance, right in front of us.

"I told you guys!!!!" Nora screeched as she jumped up and down. "It's a secret passageway!!!"

But a secret passageway to what?

"Well, I guess that would make sense. 'Secrecy' was the icon in question," Ellie said and then 'tsked' under her breath like she was expecting something much more interesting instead of just a tunnel.

In theory, this would be the point where the three of us had a continuation of the moral dilemma about whether or not we should go into the tunnel. And we would stand there arguing until some villains showed up, like bank robbers, who scared us and forced us to go into the tunnel to get away from them.

But we were in the middle of nowhere. No bank robber was going to show up.

And Nora had already walked right into the tunnel entrance.

So—yeah.

"It's dark in here guys!" she shouted back to us.

"Of course it is, you idjit. It's a tunnel," Ellie replied.

"Well, are we going to follow her?" I asked Ellie.

"If we go in, the door may close behind us and we'll be trapped inside a tunnel forever until we starve to death," Ellie said.

Oh. Yes.

An uplifting thought.

Starving to death.

"But if we stay here we won't know if that tunnel actually goes anywhere," she continued. "Although, if we're lucky, some man-eating beast lives in there and will devour Nora so she'll stop bugging us once and for all."

Oh. Another uplifting thought.

Apparently Ellie had a much darker mind than I had ever given her credit for.

"Let's go," I said. "We can't let her have all the fun

without us, whether we're trapped in there forever—or we get eaten."

Ellie and I followed Nora into the tunnel, feeling our way along the walls in the darkness. The whole thing seemed to be made out of brick, so clearly humans had constructed it, and it was not dug out by some massive groundhog.

"You don't think there's bugs in here, do you?" Ellie asked.

"*Noooooope*," I answered quickly.

That's the last thing we needed—a screaming, running, panicked Ellie in a pitch-black, confined space. She hated bugs. Like *hated*.

"Magical tunnels don't have bugs," Nora chimed in.

She must've had the same thought I did. Neither of us wanted to be trampled to death as Ellie had an anti-insect crazed episode.

"Okay, if you guys say so," Ellie whined.

Honestly, there were probably more bugs in this tunnel than in our whole garden. But I wasn't going to tell her that.

We kept walking for what felt like ages before Nora found something.

"I think I feel a ladder over here against this side of the tunnel," she sang out. "And it leads up to a latch, a handle, probably to a door or something!"

I heard a clicking sound, followed by a creaking sound.

"It's kinda heavy," Nora grunted. "I'll just push up harder against it."

And then a shaft of light poured down into the tunnel.

Nora had opened a door—but a door to what?

She scrambled up through it into the sunlight. She had no patience, and no fear, if you haven't caught on to that already.

"*This is amazing!*" she shouted down to Ellie and me. "This is the best thing ever! I can't believe where I am!"

Where was she????

Outside of the bubble????

Heaven????

A big-box store????

Ellie looked up toward Nora, glanced at me, shrugged, and then followed her up the ladder.

"You *definitely* won't believe where this tunnel led," she called down to me. "*Definitely.*"

I was excited.

Yes, it's true.

I admit that my calm, cool, collected façade was breaking down.

In fact, this was probably the most excited I had ever been in my short life. This was it. This was the moment I had been waiting for and dreaming of. I knew going up this ladder would change my life forever. No more bubble. No more lame cottage in the woods.

Instead—shopping malls, movie theaters, bakeries, farmer's markets, amusement parks, the beach, the mountains. Anywhere but this darn forest in the middle of nowhere. A new life—full of possibilities.

I climbed up the ladder.

The light was nearly blinding after the darkness of the tunnel.

Where was I going to find myself???

I got to the top of the ladder, scrambled up through the door, onto my feet, and....

"We're back at the greenhouse!" Nora shouted.

And we were back at the greenhouse.

The greenhouse.

The greenhouse.

The greenhouse.

The exact place where I had started the day's adventure.

Wow.

I tried not to show too much disgust on my face.

We had come through a hatch in the floor, which had apparently been hidden by some old lattice fencing with an ancient dusty tarp over it—which Nora had just shoved aside when she barreled her way into the greenhouse.

"The greenhouse," I said and then sighed. Deeply.

"The greenhouse! This is amazing!" Nora exclaimed, clapping.

She actually clapped. I was embarrassed for her. What was she—two years old?

"We started at the greenhouse. And now we're back. Why are you so excited when we could have just gotten here by walking out the back door of our house?" I asked.

"Well, she has a point," Ellie said, crossing her arms.

"Wait, which one of us has a point?" I asked.

I knew I had a point, for sure.

"Well, technically you both do. But for now let's dwell a bit more on Nora's excitement. The tunnel did bring us to the greenhouse. Yes, we've been here before. But that tunnel didn't end here. There is still more tunnel, it keeps going. So logic would suggest that it brings us to another building," Ellie explained.

"Another building?" I pondered. "So if we go back down there, we could end up finding ourselves in the kitchen? Where we can then—somehow—explain to Penny just how we found ourselves in this secret tunnel system, after which we might end the evening peacefully sent to our rooms without dinner?"

"It might not lead to our house," Ellie suggested. "It might lead somewhere else entirely."

Maybe to that big-box store that I had been thinking about earlier? The one with artfully displayed merchandise? And cute seasonal products?

"Ooo! Maybe it leads to an Egyptian pyramid! Or a pet store!" Nora said, clapping some more.

Those were two wildly different options.

"Probably not," Ellie replied. "But we won't know unless we go down there and keep going."

So that's what we agreed to do. Despite the fact that I was sure we'd just end up back in our own house, given the luck we were having as far as 'exciting discoveries.'

Back down into the tunnel we went, closing the door in the greenhouse behind us—although we couldn't exactly re-cover the hatch.

And then we made our way further through the tunnel, eventually finding another ladder and door. It hadn't taken that long to get to the next ladder, so we had probably made it all the way to the garage, or somewhere *equally* 'exciting,' like the tool shed.

And, unfortunately, in the dark, it felt like this was where the tunnel ended. So this was it. This was our big opportunity to discover something amazing and awesome.

Nora pushed open the door, and Ellie and I followed her once again up the ladder.

"Tsk, tsk, tsk," Eagle said to us. "I thought for sure you'd make it here faster than this."

He was sitting in an armchair, picking his teeth with his claws.

But this was a place I had never seen before.

"Where are we?" Nora asked.

"Horace's study," I answered, as the realization dawned on me.

We were in the locked study.

It had to be.

"Bingo!" Eagle answered, sort of. "Morrow wins the prize!"

"What prize?!?!" Nora asked.

"There isn't actually a prize, Norad," Ellie said, and then sighed.

"No, there isn't any prize. In fact, I would say

that there's going to be a punishment instead. A big ol' bucket of punishment," Eagle lamented, in a fake manner that annoyed the poop out of me. "Because now I'm *gonna* have to report to Penny that you guys 1) found the tunnel system 2) used magic to open it up 3) went into that tunnel system and 4) went into Horace's study, which is off-limits."

"We used magic?" I asked.

"Yes. How do you think you opened the locked door, you moron?" Eagle replied, in a 'loving' manner.

My sisters and I exchanged a glance—one that carried the meaning: 'We used magic!!!' and included a non-verbal scream.

"So, I'm going to have to tell Penny..." his voice trailed off.

"Unless..." Ellie added.

"Unless—you guys agree to make me one exotic dessert, every week, for the rest of my life," he stated, clearly proud of his blackmail plan.

"You're immortal though," Ellie scoffed.

"Exactly," he replied.

"So basically until all three of us are dead?" she asked.

"Sounds good," he agreed.

"That's a lot of pastries," Nora whispered.

"Well, not just pastries, Norad," he said. "Pastries, cookies, cakes, chocolates, candies, ice creams, brownies, strudels, muffins, macarons, tarts, creme brulees, cannolis, upside-down pineapple cakes...."

"We get the point," Ellie groaned.

"I'm not gonna make you a weekly dessert until I'm dead," I asserted.

"Fine. Fine. Then I'll tell Penny everything, and she'll seal up the tunnel system so you guys can never go back in there, and you'll never be able to come into this study ever again. And she'll probably cut off your legs, or at least revoke your TV privileges for a month—or—hmmmm," he hummed as he hopped off the chair. "Or you guys could make me the desserts, and I'll make sure that Penny doesn't know you guys are coming into the tunnel system, and coming into this study, and doing whatever you want in here—like studying magic."

He stood there.

Majestic.

Arms akimbo.

Nearly a foot and a half tall, if you included his ears.

"Deal," Nora said quickly.

"No, no deal," I said. "This is the deal: we make you the desserts, we get all that, *and* you show us how to practice magic without endangering the integrity of the force field."

"Hmmmm," he tapped his chin.

"You and Penny have been practicing magic left and right this whole time we've been trapped in here," I explained. "You guys must have some technique that prevents your magic from damaging the force field."

He squinted at me.

"An intriguing proposition," he said.

"Deal?" I asked.

"Deal," he replied. "And as a gesture of good faith, I will say that whenever Penny and I practice magic it feeds into the force field. However, she forbids you guys from practicing magic because your skills are unknown, and possibly quite volatile. It could feed the force field, or it could blow us all up. I've always been a bit curious about how your magic works though. And given the fact that you guys opened the tunnel door— something you technically should not have been able to do without an itzal izaki—clearly, there is something weird going on with you guys. Which, of course, we sort of already knew. But I still don't understand it. Also, you opening the door didn't compromise the force field. So that's promising. In return for this information, I expect my first dessert tomorrow."

Dear readers, Eagle insists on calling shadow creatures itzal izaki, their Old World name. Just so you know—itzal izaki are shadow creatures, *and* Eagle is a fussy pain in the butt.

"So you'll teach us stuff?" Nora asked.

"Sort of," he said and grinned. "Mostly it will be a series of experiments so I can figure out how your magic works without itzal izaki."

"So this is really a win-win for you, huh?" Ellie asked.

"You said it," he said, still smiling. "Then we're agreed. I get desserts. You learn how to practice magic. And I will be sure to teach you guys how to kill Verbena. Once I figure out a way to do that."

Eagle strode toward the door.

"Who's Verbena?" Ellie asked.

"Hmmmm. Well, she's the person who killed your parents, your grandparents, and your great-grandparents. She's your aunt," he explained, matter-of-factly. "You guys go out the tunnel way so Penny doesn't see you leaving through the study door. And don't touch anything in here!"

And he was gone.

Probably off to study dessert recipes.

"Our aunt?" Nora asked softly.

Verbena.

That was the first time I had heard that name. It was the first time I had heard the name of my parents' murderer. And it was the first time I had ever heard of us having an aunt.

"I wonder why she did it," Nora murmured. "Why would she kill her own family?"

She glanced at Ellie and me. Expecting an intelligent answer to a question we could barely fathom.

"Does it matter?" I asked. "According to what Eagle just said, she's probably still alive, still out there, and probably looking for us. And we have to figure out a way to kill her, which apparently even Penny and Eagle don't know how to do."

"No one knows how to do it," Ellie said. "Or else, they would've done it by now. And we wouldn't be trapped in this bubble."

"Well, *we're* going to figure it out," Nora declared.

Ellie and I stared at her, looks of discouraging disbelief on our faces.

"Well, we *have* to figure it out," I said.

"We do?" Ellie asked, in a contemplative tone.

"Do you guys want to be stuck in this bubble for the rest of our lives?" I asked. "Just watching the world through the TV and the computer? Never seeing or doing anything ourselves? We have to figure it out. We have to free ourselves. And we have to free Penny. She's taken on the role of our guardian because we don't have any family left. But don't you guys ever wonder what she gave up to be in here with us? What about her family? What about her future? Do you guys wanna watch her grow old and bury her in the back yard like a Labrador Retriever because we can't leave this darn bubble? And what happens then?"

"You're a bit morose, aren't you?" Ellie interrupted. "And I thought I was the morose one around here...."

"We are dealing with issues of life and death here, Ellie," I said. "Haven't you always felt kinda hopeless and helpless? We all know what happened to our family. And we all know that we're trapped in here because of it. But how long will hiding here keep us safe? How long do we have before Verbena comes for us? And we don't know anything about magic. We can't protect ourselves.

We can't protect Penny. We don't even know how the force field works."

"Then we should figure it out," Nora added. "For our family, for Penny. We can't spend the rest of our lives wondering when our aunt will show up, and not be prepared to do anything."

So it was decided.

We would learn about magic.

And we would learn how to make hundreds of desserts for Eagle.

And maybe in the process we'd finally learn what actually happened to our family.

CHAPTER THREE.

Morrow Explains Some Stuff.

By Morrow.

Morrow: I guess now would be a good time to explain who, or what, Eagle is. Since he's the one who's going to secretly teach my sisters and me about magic.

As previously mentioned, he's Penny's shadow creature, or itzal izaki. He's not actually an eagle, nor is he a rabbit. Although we all call him 'rabbit' to tick him off.

Eagle: I'm a springhare, dammit. *SPRING-HARE*.

Morrow: Well, yes. He *is* a springhare. A tiny, furry combination of a rabbit and a kangaroo rat. All wrapped up in a ball of animosity. Who likes to interrupt people.

Eagle: You could have at least *tried* to make me sound a bit better than that, couldn't you? You know what? I can tell this part of the story for you. It will be better that way.

Morrow: I doubt it will be unbiased.

Eagle: Oh, like your version is going to be unbiased?

Morrow: Anyway, shadow creatures are partners with the lejerdemani. Each lejerdemani has a shadow creature, and without it she or he is unable to practice magic.

Each shadow creature is immortal though, so he or she has been partnered with several lejerdemani over time.

Eagle: And if you are a fan of fiction you are invariably now comparing these itzal izaki to say....

Morrow: Whoa, whoa, whoa. Stop right there. You don't need to tell the readers what to compare the idea to.

Eagle: Well, it's gonna happen. And clearly the author is *not* that original.

Morrow: I'll have you know that the author came up with the idea for shadow creatures long before she had heard about those other shadow things made up by other authors.

Eagle: Yeah, *right.*

Morrow: You aren't helping. The main point to consider here is that there is nothing new under the sun. Which means that if you go looking for it, someone else has always already had an idea.

So the idea for the shadow creatures came out of Eagle. He just popped into the author's head one day as she was trying to write about Penny.

This snarky, bitter furry thing started taking over her mind. He was the opposite of Penny's loving, nurturing, understanding personality. Instead, he was a giant pain in the butt.

And she started researching the id, ego, and all of that personality stuff in psychology. Trying to figure out why Eagle would be such a butthole and how he related to Penny.

Eagle: I think butthole is an understatement. I work very hard to be a whole ass.

Morrow: So—um, ignore him. In her research, the author landed upon Jung's writings on the 'shadow,' which he describes as the part of a person's personality that they are not consciously aware of—the instinctual, the irrational, the negative. The stuff we try to tamp down and keep hidden.

According to Jung's theories, the shadow is necessary. The more you embrace both the positive and negative aspects of your personality, the more productive and creative you will be. As bad as the shadow might be, you need it.

And from that information the author thought: wouldn't it be funny if you had a cute, furry, physical manifestation of all the bad things about your personality that you try to keep hidden from the world?

A mean, rancorous, vain little fluffy thing that constantly harasses you and everyone you love? And if you yourself are a butthole then the shadow creature would be a sweet, happy little fuzzy thing that wants to help everyone, bring about world peace, and cure cancer. Wouldn't that be funny?

Eagle: No, not really. Whoever wrote this has a terrible sense of humor.

Morrow: As you can now tell, typically shadow creatures are a bunch of angry little jerks. Their 'spirit realm' habitat is the site of a constant out-of-control party. They are (usually) the complete opposite of a positive outward persona—lazy, violent, foul-mouthed, vile lil' buggers that act out all the negative aspects of someone's personality.

Each lejerdemani develops this interdependent, (generally) unhealthy relationship with their shadow creature, and they try to get through life one day at a time. Although their shadow creature is difficult to live with, if they want to be productive, creative, and their true self—they need to embrace him.

Eagle: Don't embrace me. Don't touch me. I'll call the cops on you.

Morrow: I didn't mean to actually physically embrace you. Embrace has more than one meaning.

And yes, dear reader, the author realizes that her incessant yammering and talking about herself in the third person while writing as Morrow will mean that if anyone does read this novel, they will probably only be able to get through it once, after which they will most likely burn this book in sheer and utter frustration.

She knows that this type of annoying commentary right here doesn't really lend itself to making this a re-readable classic.

But on the bright side, then she will become famous as the author of the book that everyone has to burn immediately after reading it. And I think that's its own publicity right there.

Anyway, back to Horace's study.

"So we should definitely touch something, right?" Nora asked, peering around like a kid in a candy shop.

"Eagle told us not to, Norad," Ellie replied.

"Yeah, but when's the last time we listened to Eagle?" she responded.

"Well, we could sort of just get the lay of the land," I said.

And with that, we began to sift and poke through everything in the room without actually disturbing anything in a way that would be noticeable.

The study had wall-to-wall bookshelves filled with books (of course), as well as paraphernalia of all kinds. Glass bottles full of weird substances. A card catalog unit—every drawer filled with colored powders. Jars full of paintbrushes, pencils, pens, feathers.

Boxes on top of cases on top of boxes. Hundreds of sacks of coins. Knickknacks, from ancient valuable stuff to cheap kitsch. Sculptures. Paintings. Dishware. Stuffed animals. It was just a random assortment of bizarre junk.

"Is that an eyeball in a jar?" Nora asked.

"I'm pretty sure there's an octopus in that tank over there," Ellie added.

"The books are the only thing I know what to do with," I said, and sighed. "Everything else is a mystery."

"Well, I know how to sit in a chair. So that's what I'm gonna do," Ellie said as she plopped down in the armchair Eagle had enthroned himself in earlier. "Let me know if you guys find anything interesting."

She grabbed the nearest book and began reading.

I started recording some of the labels of the containers into my notebook: 'Guignet's Green,' 'Gelber Ocker,' 'Nero di Vite,' 'Miel,' 'Sovereigns and Loonies,' 'Widower's Teeth.' Gosh, I hope that last one was just a nickname for something.

"It's gonna take ages to go through all of this stuff," Nora said as she sat down in another chair. "Do you think Eagle will really teach us about all of this?"

"Well, even if he doesn't—you should teach yourself. Grab a book, moron," Ellie replied.

"Hmmmmm, nice. Very nice," Nora said, and then stuck her tongue out at Ellie as she started opening the boxes on the small table next to her chair. "Look at this. There's six eight-sided dice in this box without anything else. Why would you need *six* eight-sided dice? And without a board game or anything else?"

"Maybe you'd need them if you didn't read the instructions to a certain game properly?" Ellie asked.

Instructions to what?

Honestly, I was feeling more stupid every time Ellie opened her mouth.

"A certain game?" Nora asked. "Oh, never mind. Eagle will teach us about it."

She tossed the dice back and forth in her hands, and then started rolling them on the floor.

"Well, he probably won't teach us about that, it's not magic," Ellie said.

It was at this point, as Ellie and I would learn much later, that Nora pocketed the dice as she pretended to put them back into the box and close the lid. Totally unbeknownst to her wiser and more beautiful sisters.

So much for not touching anything.

CHAPTER FOUR.

Several Unpleasant Months Later...

By Stella.

"Over here," the soft voice said.

It startled me awake.

I turned on the light and looked around my bedroom.

I was alone.

I checked my phone, my computer. They weren't on.

It was 1 am. What in the world was going on?

I opened my bedroom door and looked into the empty hallway.

Then I looked out the window. Nobody was in the driveway.

Who had said that?

Had I dreamt it?

It felt so real.

I left the light on and got back into bed, pulling my comforter up over my head.

My new normal consisted of migraines, nose-bleeds, and some light passing out.

Sometimes in public.

(Which I do not recommend.)

But hallucinating voices?

What was this??? A new level of insanity?

I fell back asleep, but….

"Die," a different voice said. "Die."

Once again I woke up. This time feeling a bit more creeped out.

I went through the whole ritual again—looking for the source of the voice.

And not finding it.

And deciding that I had dreamt it.

I got back into bed, but it took me awhile to go back to sleep.

"I'm sorry," another voice said.

I had been half-asleep.

But was now fully awake.

Was it the same voice as the first time?

It didn't really seem to match.

But it certainly didn't match with the second voice that told me to die.

"Sssssshhhhh," a voice said. "Sssssshhhhh."

And I was officially fudging-creeped-the-fudge-out.

I never went back to sleep. And that morning I arrived at school for the first day of my sophomore year feeling like a steaming pile of poo.

(Stella: Uh, Maple? Why are you scaring me with these voices??? And why did you give me this horrific mystery illness?!?!

Maple has left the chatroom.

Stella: Wait a minute. You can't just leave me here like this!

Maple is still MIA from the chatroom.

Stella: Um.)

A month-ish later I found myself sitting in my wretched homeroom, in my wretched high school at some wretched hour in the morning, sleep-deprived and questioning my very existence.

The voices from nowhere had been waking me up every night for a month.

And let's just say I was not playing the role of 'productive high school student' very well.

"Your personal statement needs to convince the committee that you have special circumstances. That you are worth their efforts," Mrs. Dimetrio lectured to us—a bunch of low-scoring misfits in this academic counseling session. "Prepare an essay draft now, while I discuss the college aptitude exams with the others."

Oh. Yes. The others.

Unfortunately, the non-low-scoring students were also hearing this. The ones with much smoother paths to college. The ones eyeballing us misfits like we had leprosy.

What was this committee about again?

I had already forgotten.

"There's a reason why they bombed the state test," one girl whispered. "Do they really think tutoring will make a difference?"

"You can't help stupid," a guy replied.

Oh. Yes.

The committee to give us stupids special math tutoring. Or not to, as the case may be. Depending on their wise judgment.

So I needed to convince some strange people that I was worth saving. I scribbled swirling lines across my notebook page to warm up my pen.

Applicant Name: Stella Grum. That much I could do. Now what special circumstances could I possibly describe?

'I am a flat-chested, black-haired, brown-eyed

girl who grew up most of her life in L.A. I somehow manage to be both pale pasty-white and tan at the same time. I'm not sure how that's possible, but it's how this freak looks.'

Why did I write that?

Because that's how you think about yourself.

What?

What?

Are you Maple?

No.

Then who are you?

The Jack Snacker of Wytney.

Uh. What??

Alright, let's pretend this isn't happening. Just keep writing.

'The last ten years of my life have been largely unremarkable except for my proclivity to accidentally give myself paper-cuts on any notebook I touch.

Also, I can never pour myself a drink without spilling it all over the kitchen counter. I guess that's also kind of noteworthy.

For the last few months, I have been quite remarkably unhealthy and prone to migraines, nosebleeds, blackouts, and passing out.

At first my father was convinced it was hormonal. Because I'm a sixteen-year-old girl who is 'developing.' Except that I have had my period since I was eleven. Sure, I am still 'developing' into a teenager, but not enough to warrant such debilitating migraines.

I mean my chest stopped growing when I was twelve, but there is really no point in waiting for that to catch up. It's not like migraines help your boobs grow.

Overall, I think I'm in the pimply-face stage of puberty. Not the stroke-like migraines stage of puberty.'

Wait, why did I write all that?!?

Because it's funny.

I ripped that page out of the notebook, crumpled it up into a ball, and shoved it down into the bottom of my backpack never to be seen again.

I started over and worked my way back to the migraines. They probably count as my special circumstances, right?

'My father took me to all the doctors. They checked me out thoroughly. Brain scans. And heart scans. Bloodwork. And more scans. And pee collecting. And more bloodwork. We tried drugs. And other drugs. And then some other different drugs. No change. In fact, the migraines might have gotten worse. You never tried smacking yourself, though.'

Uh. What?

I scratched out the last sentence, unaware as to why I even wrote it.

'And nothing was conclusive. And nothing fixed the migraines. They just kept coming. Seemingly triggered by nothing in particular. Nothing I ate, smelled, sat on, sat near, breathed in, looked at seemed to be the trigger.

By June of this year I was journaling everything I did, trying to find a pattern that led to a migraine. I never found one. Eat a kiwi after midnight. Don't eat a kiwi after midnight. Only eat avocados when the moon was full. It went on and on. I hope you choke on an avocado.'

I drew yet another line through that last sentence.

I was starting to get a bit worried about this, but I continued writing.

'It got to the point that I was afraid to eat anything. Do anything. Smell anything. Except in L.A. it's pretty impossible to stop smelling things. Smells are everywhere, on everyone, in every yard, in every building. Perfume. Cologne. Fake spray tan juice stuff. Cleaners in the public restroom. Un-bathed chihuahuas. Bathed chihuahuas.

It's a city. It smells.

Just like you.'

Why is this happening?

I sat back in my seat and tried to relax.

But my body moved forward and began writing on its own.

'By the end of July I got tired of avoiding foods, so I made you go back to eating everything. You are so annoying. You just couldn't figure out what is triggering these things. They come whenever. There is no rhyme or reason. It's probably because of me, you glorious poopiehead. So you are back to eating the way you had been eating before the migraines started. (You aren't going to stop eating avocado. We all know this.)'

What are you doing?

I'm writing your essay for you.

Who are you, really???

Your professional essay writer, duh.

No, you aren't. You're another person in my head.

'Anyway, now the migraines are worse. More frequent. More painful. We probably should be freaking out about them. But I kind of gave up hope of being able to fix the issue. This girl is naturally hopeless.'

Should I mention math somehow? How do I work that in?

I think we can loop around to it later.

I carefully put the pen down and concentrated on breathing into my nose and out of my mouth.

I don't think this essay draft is long enough. We need to keep going.

Should I panic about this? This is too weird, right? This isn't normal.

What do I do now?

Clearly I should have told my father about all of these voices that I started 'hearing' a month ago.

But you didn't want to see him freak out about it.

No, I didn't. He seemed really bothered by all this migraine stuff.

There's a reason.

What would that be?

It's a secret.

Uh. Are you the same voices I hear at night? The ones that tell me to die?

I'm one of them. I'm not sure about the other ones though.

Uh. Am I asleep right now? Is this a dream? Can't I have normal dreams where I go to an ice cream shop dressed as a giant puppy and then a pirate makes me pancakes? Like those kind of dreams. Why can't I just have those?

This isn't a dream. You are wide awake.

Am I beginning to suffer from multiple personality disorder?

No. Keep writing that essay draft though or the teacher is going to come over here and ask you why you look like a psychotic deer in headlights.

Are you someone trying to communicate with me through my dreams? Like a ghost or something?

I'm not a ghost. I wish I was. My life would be so much simpler.

'This tea tastes like pencils.'

I had just written that in the notebook. Why? I wasn't actually drinking tea. I wasn't drinking anything, in fact.

You need to write something.

'The gassy turtle.'

My hand wrote that without my control.

That's not a complete sentence.

Fine.

'The gassy turtle passes gas, gassily.'

There.

That doesn't make any sense.

'I think if I ever opened a pub I would call it

The Gassy Turtle. I suppose if I named my pub The Flatulent Chelonian that might sound super-cool and posh. But then again I don't think that name could appropriately be applied to a pub. It's not really a 'pub' kind of name.

More of a fancy restaurant kind of name. Like the kind of place with five Michelin stars and a chef from France.

(Okay, my fact-checker says that there is a maximum of three Michelin stars. But clearly my restaurant would have five because it would be that special.)'

I don't even know what a 'chelonian' is. How did I come up with that word?

You didn't. I did.

I took the pen out of my right hand with my left hand, and put it down.

And stared at it.

"Is this your journal?" Mrs. Dimetrio asked as she read over my shoulder.

When did she come over here???

I told you she was about to come over.

"Um, yes?" I said. "I mean, yes. I was just working up some ideas for the essay by journaling."

"Well, okay. But as you do that, make sure you pick out a theme and focus on it."

A theme?

"Okay," I said.

A theme? Does 'poor mental health' count as a theme?

I think it does.

Just then I stopped my insane journaling, stood up from my desk, walked up to the whiteboards, and began writing 'None of this matters.'

Over and over again.

All over the boards.

None of this matters.

None of this matters.

None of this matters.

"Amen," someone declared.

Slow clapping began at the back of the room.

Eventually most of my classmates joined in.

There were some hoots of agreement.

"Uh, Stella," Mrs. Dimetrio said. "Are you okay? This isn't like you."

I kept writing. Undeterred. Barely acknowledging her presence.

None of this matters. Over and over again.

So this was it.

This was how my time at this school ended. How could I ever come back here? How could I ever walk into this room again? Why couldn't I just blackout right now?

Go on, Stella. Pass out. Do it.

Should I fake-pass out? It's not like me passing out would surprise them. I had been doing it since the beginning of the year.

"I think we should call your father," Mrs. Dimetrio said, as she signaled to one of the front-row students, and mouthed the words 'Go get the guidance counselor' to her.

(p.s. I never did write that essay.)

CHAPTER FIVE.

Halloween.

A Road in the Middle of Nowhere.

By Stella.

I walked along the cobblestone road as the wind howled through the trees and kicked up leaves around my feet.

The crisp aroma of drying leaves filled the air.

It was usually a comforting autumnal smell for me, but not this time.

Despite it being a beautiful fall evening, I was nervous on this walk.

Someone was following me. Or something.

I couldn't see or hear them.

But the tiny hairs on the back of my neck were all electrified.

I walked quickly to outpace whatever was behind me.

The road ended at a large wrought-iron gate. It was the only entrance I could see through a monstrous stone wall that lay to either side. It was so tall and wide—looming off into the distance. It seemed to be infinite.

I had to go through the gate.

If I waited here whoever was following me was bound to catch me.

I squinted to look past the gate and farther into the woods. There was a hulking shadowy mass beyond the trees—a house. Though it looked terrifying, I knew this was where I had to go.

I pushed against the gate to see if it would open but it burned my hand when I touched it, and it didn't budge.

A sudden clap of thunder exploded around me. Lightning flashed through the sky and brought ominous clouds the color of heavy smoke.

It began to rain.

I needed to get into that house before the storm got worse.

I tried to climb up the gate.

But my hands burned if I left them on the metal for more than a few seconds.

The smell of slightly toasted skin filled my nostrils. Ew.

There had to be another way.

I took off my scarf and wrapped each end of it around my hands hoping the fabric would protect my skin. But before I could execute my new plan of climbing á la scarf, the tall bushes along the right side of the driveway started to walk toward me.

They shuffled closer and closer as if they were monsters with legs and then they shifted to the side, revealing a man standing behind them.

He stepped out of the walking bushes and extended his gloved hand to me.

"Stella," he said from behind an elaborate mask that covered his whole head. "Stella, I've been waiting for you...."

Now when a guy holds his hand out and says he's been waiting for you that can usually be interpreted as a romantic gesture.

But instead of feeling weak in the knees—a shot of fear ran up my spine like the lightning that punched through the dark sky above us.

The storm was getting worse very quickly. The wind snapped my hair around and the raindrops stung my skin like needles of ice.

This was getting to be unpleasant. In more ways than one.

The man, still holding out his hand to me,

seemed unaffected by the storm.

No rain touched him.

The wind didn't ruin his hairstyle. Not that I could see his hair from behind that mask.

It was as if he was in a storm-less bubble.

Or perhaps he was the eye of the storm itself? The peaceful-looking center point of a whirlwind of nastiness?

"Stella," he said again, walking closer. "Stella, you should come with me."

I shook my head 'no' and anxiously looked at the gate. It was all I could muster. I began to hope the gate would just open miraculously.

"Stella," the man said as he moved even closer to me, backing me up against the gate, which began to singe my clothing.

He slowly took the glove off his right hand as I desperately tried to squirm away.

As the glove came off—what I expected to see was not there.

Instead of a warm, skin-covered human wrist and hand, I saw only bone.

And before I could scream or run away, he wrapped his skeleton hand around my throat and whispered, "I knew you were the only one for me —Stella...."

"Stella," someone whispered.

I woke with a start.

My heart was pounding and my head ached like crazy.

That whole skeleton man thing had just been a nightmare.

My mother was sitting on the side of my bed, stroking my hair and whispering my name. This would have been rather comforting—except she had been dead for ten years.

I gulped and shot up, scrambling to the far side of the bed.

I had thought the skeleton man dream was pretty scary, but now I was fully awake and this was much more terrifying.

"*Mom?!?*" I said in a squeaky voice that I'm glad no one else could hear.

I kept far away from her, not sure of what was happening. She looked surprised. More surprised than me.

"You can see me?" she asked as she pointed to herself.

"Of course I can see you. You're right there, sitting on my bed! And like totally dead, if I can point that out," I squeaked.

"Ohhh!" she said as a huge smile spread across

her face. "Ohh! I'm so glad you can see me!"

"Mom, you're dead. I think if I start 'seeing' you that's a sign that I'm losing my mind. That is not a good thing."

"It's okay," she said matter-of-factly. "You're not crazy. I'm just a—a ghost."

"*Riiiiiight*, that's much more logical than Stella just being insane," I replied.

Just then my father walked into the room and my mother vanished.

"You doing all right in here, kiddo?" he asked me in a worried voice.

I was plastered against the wall next to my bed, looking petrified.

"I thought I heard you talking in your sleep and —you don't look very well. Are you okay?"

"Yeah, I'm fine. Just a nightmare. Silly thing," I lied as I could still feel my heart beating wildly in my chest.

My mother was nowhere to be seen.

Perhaps that had just been part of the dream, too?

"Well," he said and then paused briefly to stare at me with concern. "Come on downstairs. I made toast and eggs for breakfast. Then we're going to tour the Halloween parties, if you feel up to it, that is."

He looked at me pitifully.

My father lived for Halloween. Like *lived* for it. And every year we had to visit all of the Halloween festivities on this side of L.A. He usually wore a really stupid costume, and we spent the day eating a ton of unhealthy food, gathering candy, picking out pumpkins, watching parades, and getting caught up in the merriment.

After my exciting nightmare about a skeleton dude, I wasn't really that eager to go out into the world and face all of that spooky stuff.

But then there was that look on my father's face. Sigh.

He does look so pathetic.

Ah, you're back?

I never left.

Then where were you during the creepy dream and hallucination?

I was having some technical difficulties. You should probably go out with your father or he might cry. He's a big crybaby.

Um.

Go on.

So I sucked it up and spent the day Halloweening it up with my father.

And it was business as usual.

My father had not seen my mother's ghost.

Nor had he seen that terrifying skeleton man.

Life was just vanilla for him.

If only my life were so easy.

(Stella: Maple? Maple? Maple? Maple? Maple? Maple?

Maple: Gosh. You're annoying. What?

Stella: Why am I seeing my mother's ghost???

Maple: Who knows?

Stella: You're supposed to know.

Maple: Oh.

Stella: And that nightmare skeleton dude—he wasn't Archie, right???

Maple has left the chatroom.

Stella: Son of a billy goat.)

During our dinner on the pier, I thought about telling my father about this italicized voice talking to me in my head.

But then I decided that wasn't a good idea.

I also wanted to ask him about Mom and if he had ever seen her after she died—like perhaps in a ghost-like format?

But we didn't tend to talk about Mom.

So it was difficult to broach that subject.

When he did talk about her he mentioned things like....

Jeanette Valcanover-Grum:

1) Top of her class in high school and college.

2) Studying to be a veterinarian when she passed away. (Car accident. Or at least that's the lie he told me, as I learned later.)

3) So popular with the guys that she was always being asked out on dates until she met my father.

And—*of course*—he also included the normal 'parenting handbook' lingo of how she would be so proud of me.

But proud of me for what?

Stella Grum:

1) Failed almost every math class she's ever taken.

2) Barely able to move up out of middle school into high school without being held back (again).

3) Has no friends and has had the worst headaches known to man for the past six months.

Would she be proud of me for those things?

Or for having men throw themselves at me?

Okay, it was just that one guy.

And he was a skeleton.

And he tried to strangle me.

And he was in my nightmare.

Yeah. That probably doesn't count.

Sigh.

So my father and I ate while talking about mundane things. Nowhere in the conversation was there discussion of ghosts—and I just couldn't find the right moment to bring it up.

The morning after Halloween, I saw my mother's ghost again.

She was writing on the fogged bathroom mirror with her definitely dead finger as I got out of the shower.

She smiled at me and then disappeared.

And then I got back into the shower.

Yes, I eventually read what was written on the mirror as well.

After I washed the pee off myself.

"Go to the museum—alone."

The museum?

Um.

Which one?

The art museum?

Like the one on the hill?

Or some place else?

This was a conundrum.

1) I wasn't sure which museum she was talking about. Couldn't she have been more specific?

2) My father had told me to never go to any museum without him. In fact, I had been forbiddendenden—how does one spell that properly? Forboden? Anyway, I wasn't allowed to go to any museum without him.

I was the only teenager who had to be chaperoned by her father during field trips. He had been at every single one since I had started school. It was a bit ridiculous. He never told me why I wasn't allowed to go without him.

I had thought perhaps he just had a phobia about me being around old things. But really, that made no sense. He was old, and he was next to me all the time. Like: ALL THE TIME.

So my mother's ghost wanted me to go to the museum, alone.

Why?

Was she going to meet me there?

And tell me why she suddenly started showing up?

Why did it have to be at the museum?

Why did I have to be alone?

As you can tell, I overthink things a bit. So all I had were questions. A lot of questions. Where was the logic in this situation? Did a ghost really just write on my mirror? Or am I hallucinating?

But asking myself more and more questions wasn't going to help me figure out the answers. So I decided to go to the museum after school. Alone. Even though my father would have a coronary if he found out. But I was going to do it anyway. Yes.

Why?

Because you're stupid.

Um.

That's going to be the answer to many questions coming up in your head from here on out.

Uh. Thanks.

CHAPTER SIX.

Halloween.

Badger's Wood.

By Morrow.

"Hit her again!" Eagle yelled to Nora.

She sent another 'wet blanket' spell at Ellie, who didn't manage to counter it in time with her usual 'bed of roses' spell.

A pile of wet blankets dropped from the cloud above Ellie's head, which Nora was controlling, and smothered her. I was casting a protection spell though, so Ellie was essentially unharmed.

Or rather—the blankets hadn't killed her—but it was probably quite uncomfortable just the same.

"*Aaccckkkk,*" she cried out as she cast a disappearance spell on the blankets and gasped for air.

She wiped the residual moisture off her face

with her sleeve and glared at Nora, who grinned in response.

"I knew I'd get you eventually!" she yelled at Ellie, and then stuck out her tongue, for good measure.

Nora had been trying to make that spell work for several days, but Ellie was always faster casting her own spell. Which meant that Nora ended up standing in a bed of roses—her own spell blocked from being successful as she tried to avoid the plentiful thorns.

It was all a game of concentration.

You had to be able to fully concentrate on your own spell, or what you wanted to happen wouldn't happen.

You may be wondering where we were carrying out these mock battles of stupid spells.

Well, it was in the woods.

Inside another bubble.

Which was inside the original bubble.

Nora nicknamed this new bubble 'Little Sven.'

Why were we in the woods?

Good question. And me with my one-hundredth-itchy-mosquito-bite also pondered that question, daily.

Unfortunately, soon after we discovered a way

inside Horace's super-secret-locked study, Penny started using it more and more. God knows why? It's not like she tells us anything, ever. All she mumbled was something about 'work for Derek.' A dude who had apparently grown up next door to Penny, and had a daughter named Stella, according to Eagle.

Anyway, Penny's persistent presence in Horace's study meant that Eagle really couldn't use it as a base of operations for our training.

So we went into the woods, where he established 'Little Sven'—a camouflaged bubble where Penny couldn't (in theory) find us and see what we were doing.

And when I say training—I mean *TRAINING*. **All caps. Italics. Loud voice.**

Eagle was not teaching us what I had expected him to teach us.

I honestly expected endless boring lectures from him on the history of the lejerdemani, dating back to the time that dinosaurs roamed the Earth. (Don't worry—lejerdemani weren't actually around back then.)

But Eagle was not messing around. Instead we learned combat spells, defense spells, protection spells, tactical spells, survival spells, etc. It was like an Army Rangers course. He wanted us to be able to fight and survive—and kill—if we had to.

But there was one major problem with that….

<u>Some things my sisters and I have learned during the last six months:</u>

1) All magic inside the bubble (aka Sven, and even Little Sven) needs to be positive, or just not negative or evil. So any 'bad' spells have to be jokes essentially—things that are meant to be funny. If a negative or evil spell was cast inside the bubble, Penny would know right away and know the general location of where it had been cast.

So only happy thoughts are allowed here.

But, of course, Eagle is a pest and he had to be allowed to do his normal pranks, and be an annoying butt-hat, etc. Or else he'd probably break down the integrity of the whole force field with his pent-up annoyingness and anger.

So 'funny' spells were 'okay'd' to operate within the bubble system.

For example, Eagle could cast a spell to trip Penny as she walked up the stairs.

But he couldn't cast a spell to say—murder us in our beds at night.

Which I guess was comforting.

In a way.

2) Eagle figured out a way around the no-real-combat-spells-allowed rule by creating a system of comic idiom-based spells that worked like jokes.

'Wet blanket' meant that someone would be smothered by wet blankets (see previous). 'Bed of roses' meant that someone would find themselves in a bed of thorny roses (see previous).

'When pigs fly' usually ended up in someone getting pooped on by an airborne pig.

'Straight from the horse's mouth' meant that you'd force someone to feel the lovely, lovely sensation of being puked up by a giant horse head.

'Cool as a cucumber'—well, your victim would feel very, VERY cold—while looking like a human-cucumber combo thingy.

'Flea in one's ear'—pretty self-explanatory. (Although, Ellie declared that no one was allowed to use any bug spells on her after Nora tried this one out.)

I could go on and on, but you should probably have gotten the idea by now from my clearly-very-awesome skills at explaining stuff.

3) During our mock battles in Little Sven, two

of us fought, while the third would cast that protection spell I mentioned earlier. At least one of us was always in charge of maintaining that spell so no one would actually get hurt, which would give us away to Penny.

So we learned protection spells, healing spells, invisibility spells, how-to-sneak-up-behind-someone-so-they-don't-know-that-you're-coming spells. Later today we were supposed to learn—and practice endlessly (I am sure)—idiom spells that one could use to deflect a spell back onto someone.

These were not leisurely lessons. This was magic boot camp.

4) As much as we would have liked to practice all of this stuff 24 hours a day, Eagle established a hard rule that none of us were allowed to practice magic without him. Because he was the one casting a masking spell over all of our activities, hiding them from Penny.

And he also needed to be there to make sure things didn't 'get out of hand.'

Which could easily happen.

And almost did on several occasions.

Especially when someone was using the 'get your knickers in a twist' spell.

(Which was eventually banned.)

And then there is "The Really Big Thing" my sisters and I have learned these past six months:

Well, this one we kinda learned right away. It didn't take months.

Eagle had been wondering *how* our magic worked. But he already knew *why* the three of us could fully, 100% practice magic from when we were five.

It's because we're half demi-god.

Huh.

Yes, our father had been a demi-god.

He was created to serve the God of Destruction, Suntsitzea.

But unlike normal demi-gods, he was hand-crafted by Penny's grandfather, Horace Welser, and our great-grandfather, Henry Coventry—two lejerdemani—with the help of Mr. Sunny-Pants (aka Suntsitzea, if you hadn't caught on to that).

Our father was one of a group of thirteen 'Lastangs'—as Horace named them—who were created to hunt down the enemy that had been killing off lejerdemani.

(The enemy who ended up being our Aunt Verbena. But that part was a bit confusing, since Verbena hadn't existed the whole time that this enemy had been murdering lejerdemani. Or had she? Well, I'm sure I'll figure out what that's all about later, dear readers, so be patient with me.)

Back to the main point, usually demi-gods and lejerdemani wouldn't have been able to reproduce. But because my father was this unique breed of demi-god he was able to marry our mother, a lejerdemani, and produce us three freaks.

So we didn't need all of the normal stuff that lejerdemani needed to practice magic. And we didn't have to wait until we hit puberty to get our powers.

Which is probably a good thing.

Because poor Penny would've had to deal with three hyper-hormonal girls all getting magical powers around the same time, and she probably would have fled the bubble—screaming the whole way out.

CHAPTER SEVEN.

Going to the Museum.

Which I'm Not Supposed to Go To.

Don't Tell My Dad.

By Stella.

I made my way to the museum after school. The one that I could see from my house, perched upon a precipice.

(Yes, even though I'm only sixteen I do know words like precipice. Just don't ask me about the quadratic equation. Or how to spell forbiddend-enden. Forboden?)

I assumed that this was the museum in question, given the proximity to my home.

(Yes, I even know the word proximity. I spent a

lot of time studying the 'p' section of a dictionary once, okay? Don't ask why. You don't want
to know. Or if you are smart enough, you already
know why. Cough.)

I boarded the museum tram and zipped along
the hillside toward my destination.

Other people chatted and looked excitedly out
the windows. It must be nice to be a carefree tour-
ist—who isn't looking for the ghost of their very-
dead mother.

After I got off the tram, I walked across the
plaza, and into the museum lobby. I followed the
hallways to the indoor galleries and trudged along
solemnly.

My eyes floated over paintings, guards hover-
ing in doorways, statues on pedestals, and tour-
ists listening to headsets. I kept expecting to see
my mother's ghost around every corner. But she
wasn't here.

Then a woman caught my eye. She stared at me
with an air of melancholy—from inside a painting. Even though she was formed of paint, she
seemed to be judging my appearance and movements. She looked vibrant enough to open her
mouth, take a breath, and tell me her name.

I looked at her prim hairstyle with funny looped

braids, her modest black and white dress, her tiny hands, her wedding band, and then I stared back into her sullen brown eyes. She appeared too young to be married, and too sad to have ever been happy.

"Do you like it?" my mother asked me.

"The painting?" I replied nonchalantly—but then I realized who had asked the question.

My mother stood next to me, a faint translucence to her form.

I quickly looked around the room. No one else seemed to be looking at her. So was it only me who could see her?

"Yes, the painting," she said, smiling. "Do you like it?"

"Uh, yes. But she looks depressed."

"Hmmm, she probably was. Life isn't always happy."

We stared at the painting together for few more seconds in silence.

But my mind was racing.

"Are you wondering why I'm here?" she asked, still looking at the painting.

"Sort of, Mom…."

Of course, I was wondering that!!!! Duh!

"Well, I'm glad that you recognized me. That

was the first step."

"Dad, he, uh, has a lot of pictures of you around the house—although I don't really remember you."

"You were too young. We were all too young. But maybe it's better if you don't remember the past."

"I guess, but I mean—are you even real or are you some figment of my imagination? Am I dreaming this?"

She finally took her eyes off the painting for a moment and met my gaze.

"No, you're not dreaming. I'm real, well, a real ghost—and I'd like to show you something."

She turned and floated through a doorway, and I followed her into another gallery. This one had several white marble sculptures in it, one of which was buck-naked.

Unfortunately, my dead mother decided to stand/float directly in front of that one.

She didn't come back as a ghost to give me 'the talk,' did she? If so, I needed to stop her in her tracks.

"You know, Dad's already given me the birds and the bees talk, Mom," I said as I tried to avert my eyes from the naked statue.

"No, that's not what I want to talk about. Do you come to this museum often?"

"No. In fact, I'm forbidden from even coming into museums without Dad. I'm sort of breaking a big rule right now."

"Well, that's because he didn't want you to know that you're a lejerdemani."

"I'm a what?"

"Lejerdemani."

"A what?"

"I'll show you. Don't worry. Let's start in a simple manner. Look at this statue of Apollo—study the lines, the material, the texture of the marble, his facial features, the carver's skill. Look at his body, his muscles, his anatomy. It's all part of the form, the power of the art, its aura—study him."

What exactly was my mother trying to get me to do here?

Was this an impromptu from-beyond-the-grave art history lesson?

Why on Earth would that need to happen?

Or was she trying to teach me about the naked male body?

Why on Earth would that need to happen?!?!

"Go on," she insisted, gesturing toward the sculpture.

I tried to do as she said. Humoring the deceased and all.

But within five minutes I was humming some inane tune to distract myself from the sheer awkwardness of all this, and I turned away.

"Mom, I can't look at a naked guy with my dead mother standing next to me telling me to look at a naked guy—even if he is just carved out of marble."

Then someone tapped me on the shoulder.

"Yeah?" I asked, turning and looking up at the person—expecting to see a giant museum guard who would ask me to leave for talking to myself like a crazy person as I stared at some statue's wang.

"My, my. You're a lovely young woman. Where would you like to go today?" that same wangy statue said as he shifted his weight, looked at me closely, and grinned.

I stared up at him in utter astonishment.

"That statue just smiled at me," I said to the empty room.

Well—empty except for the statue, which was still looking at me.

My mother's ghost was gone. It was as if she'd never been there.

The statue blinked, waiting for me to say more.

"You're naked," was all I managed to stutter as I smiled at him like a nutter.

His right eyebrow went up.

"I'm not naked. I'm nude. The male nude, duh. It's an artistic classic. A celebration of the male form. Of the beauty of nature. I am Apollo, the ideal male. God of the sun, of prophecy, of the arts, and of mice. I am the most beautiful man ever to exist."

During this monologue there had been a lot of dramatic arm gestures and he had adjusted the crown upon his head assertively.

"You're still naked," I replied, averting my gaze.

"Hmmmm," he hummed as he pursed his lips and picked up a swath of marble from his feet that moved like it was cloth. He wrapped it over himself as he asked, "Is this better?"

"Uh, yeah."

Yep, this statue was talking to me.

Or was I just talking to myself in *Crazy Land*?

"So where would you like to go today?" he continued. "I can't even count the years it's been since one of you has visited me. I used to see droves of you. But not anymore."

"What are you talking about?"

"Lejerdemani—magical person-thingies. I used to see them in Italy and France all the time. But not here."

"When were you in Italy and France? You're a statue."

"I was carved in Venice and moved to France. I had a brief stint in the Bahamas. That was nice. And now I am here, in Cali-fornia."

"Okay, I'm talking to a statue. Am I really talking to a statue right now?"

"Of course you are, you silly thing. You are a lejerdemani. Haven't you done this before?"

"No. No, I haven't. This is all new to me. My mother's ghost just said that word to me a few moments ago, but now she's—gone. I have no idea what it meant."

"Strange. There used to be ceremonies, apprenticeships, and years of study, after which there were more ceremonies, apprenticeships, and years of study. Then you would get this fluffy animal thing, a bracelet, and some tattoos. And afterward you would spend more years studying. Boring as heck if you ask me. But you look old enough to know about all of this."

"Did you just say I look old?"

"Cough. No, absolutely not."

"Did you just say the word 'cough?'"

"Maybe. Anyway, you seem to have your powers, sort of—somehow. And I can bring you to any place that I have been so I think we should go to Venice. I have fond memories of it and it's the perfect place to explore when you're new to this game," he explained, assuredly, convincingly.

"How in the world would we go to Venice? We're in a museum on the other side of the globe."

Apollo stepped off his pedestal and held out his hand for mine.

When I hesitantly placed my palm into his, he beamed.

"Hum that tune again," he said.

"What tune?"

"The one you were humming before."

"But I don't remember it."

"Alright. I see you *are* a novice. Close your eyes. Clear your mind. And then think of me," he said slyly as he winked at me.

What a pompous weirdo.

But I thought of him just the same. I couldn't help it. It's like when someone tells you not to laugh and then you can't help but dissolve into hysterical giggles.

Apollo. Apooollo. A-p-o-l-l-o. God of the sun, of

silly crowns, of nakedness, of soft cream-colored marble, and of mice.

And then I was humming, note after note, the tune falling up and down like a pleasant waltz.

I closed my eyes for a split second and when I opened them I was in what appeared to be a stone carver's studio, surrounded by chunks of marble in various stages of sculptural-completion.

Apollo was next to me, dancing in rhythmic circles, and strumming a tiny harp.

"Oh, how I love Venice!" he sang.

This had to be a hallucination, a nightmare.

I was probably passed out cold on the museum floor, or being taken to a hospital, and this was just my damaged brain playing horrid little games with me.

"*What just happened?!?!?*" I asked, panicked.

"We went to Venice. Duh."

"But how?"

"Your magic combined with my magic and we traveled together to Venice! Wheeee!!!"

"My magic? What? Why?" I groaned.

"I thought you wanted to come here," Apollo asked, as if he hadn't just contributed to the issue at hand.

"How?! *How did I make that happen?!*"

"By humming the song, my song, and holding my hand—it triggers the magic. It's like a spell. Duh—again."

"Ughhh. Why did I hum that thing?! Quick, hold my hand and let me hum the song again. *I don't want to be in Venice!*" I whined as I offered him my hand.

"Why don't you want to be here?" he asked with an injured tone, as he made no movement to take my hand.

"I can't just be popping in and out of places when I don't have the ability to control it! Also, I'm pretty sure I'm having hallucinations from a stroke right now, so I'd really like to go home."

"Too late!" he said, smiling. "We're here and we're staying!"

"*Ugh!*" I groaned as I sat down on the floor and started to think about Apollo again in an attempt to remember the song.

"What are you doing?" he asked.

"Sun, harps, mice," I said.

"It won't work."

"Why not?"

"We have to work together. Because you're not trained enough, and hence not powerful enough, to do it on your own. You don't even have one of those furry magical beast things with you. So if I don't *allow* you to tap into my strength you can't go anywhere. That's how it works with *magicae statuas*."

"With what?"

"*Magicae statuas*—magic statues. Made by the lejerdemani. They often use Latin to say stuff. Or Basque. Or Italian. Or whatever else weird language they feel like using."

"Magic statues," I repeated.

How did my brain come up with magic statues for a hallucination?

Is it secretly a really creative brain?

Probably not.

"Right. Magic statues. Made by the lejerdemani. Right," I said. "Again, what the heck is a lejerdemani?"

"Um," Apollo said and then stared at me for a moment. "*You* are a sort of subspecies of humanity that has magical abilities, which normally develop when the person is an adolescent. A time when a lot of things are developing. Tee-hee. And you guys usually have a furry creature thing that follows you around. You really don't know this?"

"No. How could I? I don't even know how to spell that lejer-something-word."

"This is unique. I've never had to explain this to someone before. So, um. Let's see. Your magical abilities are designed so that the lejerdemani can assist the gods in their duties and obligations—if the gods ask for help that is. Some lejerdemani live their whole life never being called upon to assist a god. Other lejerdemani families serve a god for generations."

"Sounds totes legit. I'll just call my Dad and tell him what's going on. He'll fly over here, scream at me, and then beat you into a fine dust. Then maybe he can explain about lejerdemani and magical statues to me, or just have me committed to a mental hospital. Which is probably the more likely outcome."

I fumbled through my bag to find my phone.

Apollo looked at me skeptically.

I found the phone, but there was no signal. Son of a monkey.

"Doesn't Venice have cell phone tower thingies?" I asked, frustrated.

"Not 1781 Venice," Apollo said.

"Not what?"

"There are no phones in Venice in 1781."

His tone definitely implied that the phrase 'you moron' was tacked on to the end of his statement, although he hadn't said those words.

"Have we seriously somehow traveled in time as well as across the globe?!?!" I asked.

He nodded.

I got up from the floor and scurried over to the nearest open window, which looked out over a canal, crowded with narrow boats. People shuffled along a stone walkway wearing clothing that was *not* from the 21st century.

"Wait a minute," I said to Apollo, who had now grabbed a polishing cloth from a bench, and was rubbing himself down as if he were at a refreshing spa. "What year did you say this is?"

"1. 7. 8. 1," he sang to me as an answer.

I looked out the window once more.

No motorboats. No electric or phone wires. No satellite dishes. No sounds of car engines. Not one single person carried a phone or had ear buds plugged into their heads. There was nothing modern in this world at all.

It looked like calling my father to come get me wasn't going to be an option.

I turned back and glanced around the room—hoping to see someone who might help me, but there was no one here.

"Where is everyone?" I asked. "Why is this

whole place empty? What are all the stone carvers doing?"

"It's carnivale. 'What *aren't* they doing?' is a better question," Apollo answered playfully.

"Are you sure we're in Venice and this isn't just some nightmare my brain made up??"

"Hmmm," he pursed his lips and studied me quizzically.

Then he scooped up a heaping handful of marble dust from a nearby tabletop and blew it in my face.

Nice.

Thank you.

"When we get back to Cali-fornia you will still have some of that dust in your hair," he announced matter-of-factly. "That is, unless we go bathing together."

He probably winked at me then, but I couldn't see it.

I was too busy coughing, hacking, and trying to wipe the dust off my face.

"So we *are* going back?!" I managed to inquire eventually, in between gasps for dust-free air.

"Of course. *After* I find Eurydice. Do you think I want to stay in 1781 Venice forever? Do you know how badly this place reeks in the summer? That's not just water in those canals you know."

"Um, *eww*. Wait—do statues even have a sense of smell?"

"Yes. I have a sense of smell, thank you very much. In fact, I can do anything you can do, only better. Including smell things!"

He beamed.

I rolled my eyes.

"Well, can you even bathe without sinking? You must weigh a ton."

"Thanks for the compliment," he said sarcastically. "I can bathe just like you, it just has to be... shallow water."

It was the first time in the history of humanity that a conversation like this had ever taken place. I was sure of that. But before I started picturing him bathing, I decided to change topics.

"So who is Uri-something and why do we have to find her?" I asked.

"The real Eurydice is a story for another time, but hopefully you already know it," he said and then looked at me for confirmation.

I didn't have a clue what he was talking about.

He emptied his lungs with a pained sigh.

"What *do* they teach you children nowadays? *My* Eurydice is another statue that was carved by my

Master in this shop. I fell in love with her and I'd like to bring her back with me to Cali-fornia."

He really couldn't say that word without tripping on it.

"Can we actually bring things back with us, through time?"

I couldn't believe I was asking that question. It sounded like a line from a 1980s sci-fi B movie that only three people saw.

"Oh yes. As long as the mass of the object is not larger than the mass of you and me combined. We can't just place a hand on the Basilica San Marco and it will just join us inside the museum when we go back."

The Basilisk-san-what?

I decided to skip that question for now and opt for a different one.

"So where is this statue now?"

"She should be right here, where I left her!" he said excitedly.

He began shuffling from sculpture to sculpture, gazing at them briefly, looking for his love.

After checking every single item in the room twice, he declared, "She's not here."

"Oh, well. That's too bad. You'll just have to stop by some other time. If we leave now, I'll still be home in time for dinner," I remarked cheerily.

"What? *No way*. I'm not leaving here without her. Do you know how long it's been since I came into contact with one of you? I've lived without Eurydice for hundreds of years. It was stupid of me not to have returned for her before when I had the opportunity. Lejerdemani are like an endangered species now. You've all gone off somewhere or died. Who knows. If we don't get her now, I may never get the chance again."

His words rang with sincere desperation.

So desperate in fact, it kind of made my stomach hurt.

"You're not magically powerful enough to come and go through time by yourself?" I asked.

"Of course not! We need a lejerdemani to do that. Do you think I'd be standing in museums all my life if I could just be running around on my own? We are only able to *move* when a lejerdemani sings or hums our song. Or magically activates us through a variety of spells—all of which are much too complicated for someone like you."

"Wait. Does that mean you can still see and hear things all the time though?" I asked the question before I even considered if I actually wanted to know the answer.

"Yes, of course we can."

Oh.

Creepy.

Super-creepy.

Like—creepy.

"But not all statues are magical. Just like not all paintings are magical," he continued. "Only objects created by the lejerdemani are magical. So your porcelain princess figurine on your nightstand is most likely not watching you in your sleep."

Good to know.

Not that I had a princess figurine…cough.

"Is there a way to tell if something is magical?" I inquired, wondering if I could scan my house for things that are actually 'alive,' so-to-speak.

Though perhaps that wasn't really a good idea.

"Yes. You concentrate your mind on that object and a song pops into your head. You automatically hum it like the idiot *you* are and then it will come to life before your eyes. Then you can tell you've found one."

I rewarded his frank answer with an uneasy half-smile.

"But don't worry," he continued. "Most magical objects have not survived the tests of time. When they're destroyed they go to a different Realm. Paintings and sculptures are treasured art objects though, so in a way we are immortal. Humans and lejerdemani spend a lot of time, energy, and money trying to preserve us. If you don't eat magical food it will eventually rot and smell pretty bad. But you can stare at a beautiful marble sculpture forever. I never spoil."

He threw another smile my way and gracefully motioned toward himself.

Magic food?

There's such a thing as magical food???

What in the—well, never mind about that for now.

Even though Apollo was full of himself, he was answering all of my questions and telling me a lot of things I hadn't known.

I felt like I needed to return the favor.

"Alright. Although you aren't going to give me much of a choice, I have decided to help you find Uri-dee-cee. If she isn't in this room, maybe she's in a different one?" I suggested.

"Good idea!" he said as he darted out of the doorway and across the hallway.

Zipping in and out of room after room, he had soon scouted the entire first floor of this building.

"She's not here," he said and then sighed. "We'll have to go ask Casanova where she went."

"Are you telling me we're going to go talk to the *real* Casanova, or a statue of Casanova?"

I recognized the name as someone famous—although for what I had no idea.

(Casanova wasn't in the 'p' section of the dictionary, okay?)

"The real Casanova. Who would make a statue of him?" he replied, dumbfounded. "I know where he'll be. He has a normal hangout."

He moved to exit the room.

Nervousness shot through me as I thought about what lay beyond these walls.

"We can't go out into the streets of Venice as a 21st century girl and a marble statue," I said.

"Well, it's carnivale, so they won't take a second glance at me. But you, Sweet Zeus. You stand out like a—let's find something for us to wear."

I was grateful that he had cut off his own sentence. I wasn't the kind of person who wanted to stand out at all, anywhere, at anytime, or any place.

"I saw some clothes in the other room, I'll grab those and we can be on our way," he added.

"Wait, wait," I said as I grabbed his arm. A horrid

thought had loomed in my mind. "Uri is magical too, right? I'll be able to make her move and walk, just like you?"

"Yes, she's like me. Her song is a little different, but she'll walk and talk just like me."

Thank goodness. I wasn't eager to get arrested in 1781 Venice for stealing someone's statue. If she could act like Apollo, then we'd just have to dress her up like a human and walk her out of wherever she was.

"Grab three outfits!" I told Apollo.

Then I silently congratulated myself for thinking ahead.

He left the room and came back moments later with long black cloaks, hats, and masks for us to wear. I felt uneasy putting the hat and mask on. It reminded me a little bit of what the skeleton man wore in my nightmare. But when I was finished dressing, everything but my sneakers was hidden. It was a good disguise.

Apollo and I exited the building. He walked along the narrow Venetian pathways with nonchalance.

I followed behind him, trying to look casual. But I was terrified.

I kept looking around in a panic.

Everything was so different here—the sights, smells, sounds.

I was scared someone would notice me, notice that I didn't belong here.

Just keep walking, Stella. Just look ahead.

We rounded a corner and spotted a donkey eating some hay by a large cart.

"Here he is," Apollo said as he pointed to the donkey.

"Here who is?" I asked.

"Casanova," he replied as he walked over to the animal.

"*Casanova is a donkey?!*"

"Yeah, what else would he be?"

"My owner has a sense of humor," the donkey interjected in between chewing.

"He just spoke," I said.

My eyes widened to the point where they were in danger of exiting my skull.

"Yes, he did," Apollo replied, nodding. "Hello my good friend, do you know what happened to Eurydice?"

"Yeah. I carted her over to the Mint last week," the animal replied.

"That donkey is talking," I said.

"Of course he's talking. All animals can talk in

my presence. I'm a god, remember?"

"Oh, yeah."

"Who is this?" Casanova asked.

"Eh, I actually don't know what her name is."

"Yes, you were too busy talking about yourself to ask," I replied.

"Well, you can tell me now. Or not, it's up to you. It really doesn't matter to me either way," Apollo said.

"My name is Stella Grum. Nice to meet you, Casanova the Donkey. Thank you for your help," I said graciously, while ignoring Apollo.

"She may not be very smart, but she is nice," Casanova remarked.

"Yes—she does have that going for her, at least," Apollo said. "Let's get going. The Mint isn't that far from here."

He started walking away.

I patted Casanova on the head and then followed him.

The Mint. I wondered what that was.

"Do they sell chocolate mints at the Mint or just, like, peppermints?" I asked as we crossed over a bridge.

"*Really???*" he asked—like I had just posed the stupidest question in the history of the world.

I decided to keep my mouth shut until we got to our destination.

We walked along a huge canal and then turned to cross a large square that was bordered by the most beautiful buildings I had ever seen.

Apollo paused—waiting for me to catch up to him as I stared in wonder.

"This is the Piazza. That over there is the Palace of the Doge. You don't want to mess with him. That is the Basilica San Marco. And that is the Mint, where we're going," he explained while pointing in various directions.

I spotted several little cafes on the Piazza as well. My stomach growled in response. I had some snacks in my bag, but how often do you get to eat at a café in Venice, especially in 1781?

"Can we stop and eat something?" I asked.

"No. I don't eat. I mean—I can eat, but I don't need to eat. I'm a statue, remember?"

"But I eat. I need to eat. I'm so hungry. It's always you, you, you."

He turned to me.

I could see his blank white marble eyes squinting at me from behind his mask.

"This is almost over. I'm about to find Eurydice after hundreds of years spent thinking about her.

Then we can go back to the museum. And *you* want to stop for *biscotti*?!"

It did sound ridiculous when he said it like that.

Why did I want to spend more time here than I had to?

Maybe because it was actually quite marvelous.

Apollo continued walking over to the Mint with a little skip in his step.

A woman on a stage in the middle of the Piazza began to sing some opera song thingy—very badly. The sound stung my ears, and brought tears to my eyes.

"*Aaggghhhhhhhh*," a man sitting at a café table on our left groaned. "These people don't know how to sing. It pains me just listening to them!"

Just as Apollo and I were about to walk toward the doors of the Mint, that man stood up, and walked in front of us.

He coughed and bowed deeply.

"It's a pleasure to make your acquaintance," he said and then straightened up into a dramatic pose like he was introducing himself to the King and Queen of France.

"My name is Tiziano, and this is my companion —Girolamo."

He gestured to another man, who was just getting up from the table. He had a plate of biscotti in front of him. Son of a—so darn tempting. I honestly thought about grabbing one.

But then I noticed that Tiziano was dressed almost exactly like the skeleton man. Even his mask was similar. He could have been the same exact man, except he had flesh and muscles. I looked closely at Girolamo. He was also dressed in an elaborate outfit. Was this normal Venetian attire? If so—what was I wearing? A nun's habit or something?

I turned around to study the other people in the Piazza.

Most of them were wearing something strange. While a few people here and there were dressed in black outfits like Apollo and me, the rest of the population looked like circus performers. Everyone wore a mask.

And off in the distance, I saw a group of clowns perform a mock battle with knights around a dancing bear. What the?

I pulled on Apollo's sleeve.

"What's going on here? Why do all of these people look nutty?"

"I told you. It's carnivale. This is normal," he replied quietly.

He pointed to a group of revelers.

"There go the Seven Sins. The thief is envy, the prostitute lust, the lunatic gluttony, the miser covetousness, the lawyer pride, the doctor sloth, the demon wrath. All costumes. Everyone picks a character and tries to play the part. But you have to be careful, because there are true criminals in amongst the actors."

Then he glared at Tiziano, who was still standing in his weird bowing pose, one foot in front of the other, arms flung out into the air.

"What do you want?" Apollo asked. "We are very busy people without extra time to chat."

"Well, while you may be busy—you may want to know that you're being followed by agents of the Inquisition," Tiziano replied. "They're still keeping their distance, so I doubt that they can hear us. But they'll make their way closer soon enough."

"Who *isn't* being followed by an agent of the Inquisition? In this town—they follow everybody," Apollo said to Tiziano in his normal carefree voice.

"Still, you wouldn't want to be arrested. Perhaps your companion's footwear is too unconventional and draws their attention," Tiziano added.

I looked down. My sneakers looked nothing

like what these two men were wearing on their feet. Then I glanced around us into the crowds of people, trying to spot these agents who were supposedly following us. I couldn't see anyone who was looking at us. Not when there was still a dancing bear to be watched.

"Whatever," Apollo dismissed the man's comments and stepped around him.

"But…" I began.

"C'mon," Apollo said to me, taking my hand.

My heart skipped a beat as we continued walking toward the Mint's doors. Was this a good time to bring up the fact that Apollo was the first man to hold my hand besides my father? Wait. Did it count if he was a statue?

"If you are looking for something in the Mint, we can be of service," Tiziano spoke again. "We are very familiar with its layout."

"Why—are you trying to steal something from it?" Apollo asked as he turned to look at Tiziano.

My mouth dropped open. Good thing I had a mask on to hide it. We were the ones who were trying to steal something!

Tiziano threw out a fake laugh.

"We've just been in the building before, once or twice," Girolamo finally spoke.

Apollo studied them.

"Fine. Can you show us a way to get in without attracting the attention of the guards?"

"*What are you doing?!*" I whispered toward Apollo's ear after squeezing his hand, which I was still holding.

"These gentlemen want to help us. Or so it seems. Plus, I am less afraid of these strangers than I am of the Mint guards," he said.

"Why would anyone guard a mint shop?" I asked him quietly.

He stared back and said nothing.

"There's a secret staircase hidden behind the bell tower," Girolamo said. "It leads to the officials' rooms in the Mint. What exactly are you trying to find?"

I looked at Apollo and shook my head 'no.'

"A statue. Of Eurydice," he said.

Ugh. Why couldn't he have just said 'nothing' and ignored these guys? I didn't trust them. I couldn't even see their faces or read their expressions behind those gaudy masks.

"A sculpture would be in the officials' private gallery—most likely. But it's always locked," Girolamo replied.

"Well, then we'll just have to unlock it," Apollo

said. "Show us where the staircase is."

Girolamo and Tiziano exchanged a quick glance, and then motioned for us to follow them.

We walked away from the front doors of the Mint and proceeded farther back around the side of the building. Then we took a quick right and snaked our way through several tiny passageways next to a giant tower, which I assumed was the bell tower they had mentioned. We reached a dead-end, boxed in amongst the solid walls of the buildings around us.

Girolamo pushed against part of the stone wall to the right and it shifted inward.

"How did you guys know this was here?" I asked.

Girolamo looked at me and shrugged. Tiziano quickly went through the open doorway and Apollo followed him. Girolamo gestured for me to follow Apollo, but I had visions of Mint guards or Inquisition agents lying in wait for us on the other side.

I had no idea what an Inquisition agent was, but if they could arrest you—I didn't want to meet one. But I also couldn't stand by an entrance to a secret passageway forever. That would certainly grab someone's attention.

I hesitantly walked through the dark doorway,

and saw Tiziano and Apollo climbing up equally dark stairs directly in front of us.

I followed them slowly, as Girolamo pushed the door closed behind us.

Eventually the four of us reached the top of the stairs where there was a small room with three doors.

"The door on the left leads to the hallway and the main staircase," Girolamo explained. "The one in the middle leads to the officials' rooms. And the door on the right leads to their private library. The private gallery is hidden beyond the library."

"Does everyone in Venice know all of this or is it just you guys?" I asked.

Girolamo shrugged again.

"What's in this for you guys?" I continued. "Why are you so willing to lead us here?"

"Who wouldn't want to see the officials' private art gallery?" Tiziano asked, playfully—but even a moron could tell he wasn't being truthful.

"It doesn't matter what they want," Apollo said. "Who cares why they're helping us. We just need to find Eurydice."

He grabbed my hand and opened the door to the library. We walked into a narrow two-story room lined with bookcases on both levels. It had a tiny spiral staircase that led up to a balcony on the second level. (I guess someone who isn't scared of heights could go up there and retrieve books—not me though.)

In the center of the room was a massive wooden display case where several leather-bound books sat quietly waiting for someone to read them. I looked around the room, studying each corner and bookcase. The only door in this room was the one we had just walked through. I didn't see any entrance to an art gallery.

"What do we do now?" I asked. "I don't see any more doors out of this room."

"The door to the art gallery is hidden on the second level," Tiziano said as he walked up the tiny spiral staircase to the balcony.

Ugh. I *just* thought about how I didn't want to go up there!

"Okay, let's go," Apollo said following him and gesturing to me.

I watched Tiziano walk casually along the balcony, running his hand along the woodwork of the bookcases.

"I heard there is a latch to the hidden door up here somewhere," he said.

These guys hear an awful lot of stuff.

"After you," Girolamo said as he motioned to the spiral staircase.

Oh my. This was going to be awful.

I started up it like a normal person. But was soon on my hands and knees, crawling my way from stair to stair.

"Are you alright?" Girolamo asked.

"I'm fine. I don't like spiral staircases, nor heights, nor stuff that can kill me."

I managed to claw my way to the top of the stairs, but I couldn't bring myself to stand up when I reached the balcony.

I kept crawling along, trying to get closer to Apollo. I gripped every crack and dent in the floor as if my life depended on it. I knew I was making a mess of my clothing, and that I looked like a total idiot. But my heart was pounding, my palms were sweating, and I was so scared.

"I found the latch!" Tiziano declared.

Out of the corner of my eye I saw him lift up a piece of decorative wooden curlicues on a bookcase about six feet in front of me.

A grinding noise came from behind the wall, and the bookcase shifted backward, and then began to slide to one side.

He had found the doorway. Or perhaps he had

just known where it was all along?

Once the bookcase had moved aside enough he slipped through the opening and out of sight.

Despite the slowness of my mode of transit (crawling), I eventually caught up to Apollo. He stood waiting for me by the doorway. I wanted to grab his legs in joy and to help steady myself. But he looked down at me with such disdain and said, "You are ridiculous. I can't bring you anywhere."

So much for warm comfort from him.

"Let's follow Tiziano through the bookcase," Girolamo said from behind me.

Apollo ambled forward. I crawled slowly after him. And eventually Girolamo followed us into the next room. He helped me to my feet, and started to wipe the dust from my cloak.

"Thanks," I said as I looked up at him.

Then he stopped—probably realizing that while he was helping to clean my outfit he was essentially pawing me.

"Uh. Sorry. Yeah," he stammered and turned away.

As I straightened myself out, I looked around the room. No windows. No doorways. And there was nothing in the room except a large tiered stone fountain that was set against the farthest wall.

It had a stone tortoise perched on top of it that stared at us with an air of condescension.

"*Is this the private art gallery?!*" I asked, completely shocked. "There's nothing in here except a tortoise!"

"No," Tiziano said. "This is not the gallery. It's the anteroom. We must now figure out how to open the gallery."

"You guys have been here before," I stated and crossed my arms.

"Yes," Girolamo said as he slid the bookcase door closed behind us. "Yes, we've tried to get into the gallery before."

"But we haven't had any luck," Tiziano said as he dropped his shoulders and tilted his head to the side like a sad clown.

"But I think you can figure it out," Girolamo added, pointing at me.

Why me?

"What?" I asked.

"We think you can figure out how to open the way to the gallery," Tiziano said.

"And how do I do that?"

Girolamo dug into a bag that hung at his waist and pulled out a tiny turtle shell.

He handed it to me.

"Place that top side down on top of that fountain and spin it."

"*What?*" I asked, totally clueless per usual.

"Eh. Eh. Eh," Apollo said as he grabbed the turtle shell from my hand and looked at the two men. "You two know something you aren't supposed to know."

Girolamo and Tiziano looked at each other.

Girolamo started to speak but Tiziano placed a hand on his chest to stop him.

"Yes, we know that she is a lejerdemani," Tiziano said.

"Well, in order for you to know that, you have to be a lejerdemani, too," Apollo said.

"That's true. And we are, sort of," Tiziano replied.

"Well, if you are—sort of—then you can open the door yourselves. You don't need her," Apollo said.

"We aren't the *right kind* of lejerdemani," Tiziano answered.

"There's only *one kind* of lejerdemani," Apollo said. "So what does that make you?"

"Here's the thing—the fountain is a magical portal created by the Goddess of History," Girolamo said, interrupting what I can only assume was about to become a fierce staring contest between Tiziano and Apollo. "She's got this lock on it, and we can't open it."

"Why would Mint officials have a magical portal to their art gallery that was created by the Goddess of History?" I asked—really, really confused. Like more confused than confusion itself.

"Because it's not the Mint officials' art gallery," Girolamo said. "It belongs to the Goddess of History. It's one of her secret galleries."

"It may not be the gallery you thought it was," Tiziano added. "But I can assure you that Eurydice is behind that fountain. We saw her get delivered to the Mint last week, and this is where she would be stored."

"Hmmmm. You guys are clearly not associated with the Goddess of History. Or else you'd know how to get through the door. But yet you want to get into that room. Why is that?" Apollo asked.

"Let's just say she stole something from us and we want to get it back," Tiziano said.

"And what would that be?" Apollo pushed.

"A painting. She stole a painting from me. That she shouldn't have. And I really, really need to get it back," Girolamo said.

Apollo studied the men for a moment, and then

he looked at me.

"And you guys think she can open the door?" Apollo asked.

"I think she can," Girolamo said.

Tiziano flicked his hand through the air, as if to gesture 'who knows?'

"She's certainly powerful. It is worth a try," he said.

This was all becoming very suspicious.

I wasn't powerful.

I occasionally had very powerful gas.

But I myself was not powerful.

Wait, why did I have to tell you about my bad gas?

Ignore that part.

Apollo looked down at the turtle shell in his hand, and glanced back at me.

If we didn't find Uri-dee-cee, Apollo was not going to go back to Cali-fornia. And supposedly, she was behind that fountain. This was the only way to go home. And I really, really wanted to go home.

I was starting to get really hungry.

Now I was craving biscotti *and* avocados. Well, not together as one dish. Two separate things. But. Yeah. Cough. Biscotti and avocados would be gross together, right? Well, anyway, where was I?

Oh, yes—I made the decision to get the heck out of here as fast as possible.

I took the turtle shell from Apollo's hand and walked over to the fountain. I placed the shell top side down and spun it on the highest tier. The shell began to glow a warm brown color as it turned round and round.

A sharp pain split through my head.

My headache had returned.

What fun.

My eyes closed from the pain, and I reached out for Apollo's hand. Girolamo jumped a little bit as I grabbed his hand by accident.

"Oh, sorry. My eyes were closed," I said as I let go of his hand.

Apollo stepped closer to me and took my hand.

"Are you okay?" he asked.

"I get these headaches," I said.

"Oh," Apollo replied, letting me lean against him.

Out of the corner of my eye I saw Tiziano briefly glance at Girolamo, who was busy staring at the fountain.

Water had been trickling out of the mouth of the tortoise and down the levels of the fountain, but once the shell had changed colors the water stopped flowing. A ticking sound began somewhere from deep inside the fountain.

Apollo and I took a few steps back.

Was this thing going to explode?

Several of the stones that ran along of the edges of the fountain began to rotate, as if they were gears on axels. The underside of those stones soon came into view. Each of them featured a carved image.

Girolamo stepped forward and studied the stones.

"The fool. The chariot. The Sun," he said. "22 in total. These are the Major Arcana of the Tarot."

Like those cards that the crazy lady who lives above the vegetarian restaurant reads for people? That tarot?

I looked up at Apollo to see if he understood what was going on. He was nodding in agreement but didn't say anything.

When the stones stopped rotating, a tiny piece of paper started to inch out of the tortoise's mouth. Like it was being fed out of a miniature printer.

Tiziano grabbed the paper and read aloud, "The Bull attacks the Ram. The Goat eats the Fish. The

Lion walks on the Scorpion. Or perhaps it is all the other way around?"

"What in the world does that mean?" I asked.

"It's a riddle or a puzzle," Girolamo said. "The Goddess of History loves those kinds of things. Though she's not really very good at them."

"There aren't any bulls or rams or scorpions in these images," I said looking at the stones.

"Well, like I said—it's a puzzle, but not a very good one," Girolamo replied. "According to the reading of the Tarot by the Hermetic Order of the...well, never mind about that. Let's just say that some people have matched each of the Major Arcana of the Tarot with an astrological meaning."

"They have?" Apollo asked.

"Oh, yes," Tiziano confirmed.

"In what century did that happen..." Apollo's voice drifted off as he scratched his chin.

"Do you know a lot about this stuff?" I whispered to him.

"No, apparently not," he said.

"Come on my comrade," Tiziano said to Girolamo as he slapped him on the back. "We can figure this one out. The Bull attacks the Ram. Bull —well, that's Taurus, which is the Hierophant."

"Ram is Aries, the Emperor," Girolamo continued. "The Goat eats the Fish. The Lion walks on the Scorpion. Capricorn, Pisces, Leo, Scorpio. The Devil. The Moon. Strength. And Death. The Hierophant attacks the Emperor. The Devil eats the Moon. Strength walks on Death."

Ever feel like the stupidest person in a room?

I mean, I usually felt like that in any math class —or any classroom, really.

But being around complete strangers and feeling like a total dolt? That was new to me.

How did these guys know all of this stuff? Is this what you learned as a magical lejerdemani person?

If this is the information I need to know, why had I learned algebra? What was the point of that?

Okay. I admit that I hadn't really ever learned algebra. But theoretically—what would be the point of learning it if I needed to know about devils eating moons instead???

"Uh huh," Apollo said to Girolamo. "And what do we *do* with that knowledge?"

"Press down on those stones in that order like they're buttons or something?" I asked.

That seemed too simple though.

"We can try," Tiziano said as he reached for the

Hierophant stone, or what I assume was the Hierophant stone—because I had no clue what a Hierophant looked like.

"No, no, no," Girolamo blocked Tiziano's hand from touching the fountain.

Tiziano flinched for moment in a weird way.

"The instructions also said: 'Or perhaps it is all the other way around?' I think it's meant to be done backwards. The Emperor attacks the Hierophant. The Moon eats the Devil. And Death walks on Strength."

I was officially lost.

"Touch the Emperor stone," Girolamo said to me. "Wait, what's your name?"

"Stella," I answered—in the way one answers that question when someone asks it—like immediately, without hesitation.

But Apollo quickly squeezed my hand.

"I'm not sure you should have told him that," he whispered to me.

Was I supposed to be keeping my name a secret? When did that become a thing?

"Go on, touch it," Tiziano encouraged me, pointing.

So I touched it. The stone. With the Emperor image on it—some dude enthroned.

But nothing happened.

"Do you have a signature pigment? Or a power bracelet?" Girolamo asked me.

"A what? A who?" I replied.

"She's *very* weird," Tiziano said, with a curiously sly tone to his voice.

"Okay, okay. A new approach," Girolamo said as he dug into his pocket and produced a small brown leather bag. "This contains a black pigment. One of the oldest and most powerful ever used by any lejerdemani. Put your hand into the bag, and then touch the pigment dust to each of the stones."

"A black pigment?" I asked. "Like eye shadow?"

All three men looked at me blankly.

"Like makeup?" I asked.

"Yes, sort of like makeup," Girolamo answered.

"Which pigment is it, exactly?" Apollo asked him as he held my hand back, stopping me from reaching into the bag.

"Carbon black," Girolamo replied.

"So—soot?" Apollo asked.

"Yes, soot, basically," Girolamo said as he held up the bag in front of me.

"You want me to put my hand in a bag of fireplace ashes?" I asked.

"Yes," he responded. "Sort of."

Apollo put his hand into the bag first and rubbed the pigment between his fingers, studying it.

"It is what he says it is, go on," he said to me—motioning that I, too, should put my hand into the bag.

"Do you think this will work?" Tiziano asked Girolamo.

"Well, we can only try," he answered.

So then everybody stared at me. Waiting.

Which did make me feel slightly uncomfortable.

So I stuck my hand into the bag.

The black powder was iridescent, smooth and quickly coated my whole hand.

"Is it supposed to do that?" I asked. "I hope this isn't toxic."

"It, uh—it can do that, sometimes. But d-don't worry, it's not toxic," Girolamo stuttered, looking over at Tiziano, who crossed his arms and sucked in his breath.

What did that mean?

So was it supposed to do that or not?

My headache throbbed—just to let me know it was still there.

No, I hadn't forgotten about you, giant pain in

my head.

"Okay, well go on," Apollo said to me. "We haven't got all day."

I rubbed my left temple with my clean hand, and touched the Emperor carving with my soot-covered hand. The engraved image glowed a warm orange color.

Each stone vibrated underneath my hand as I touched it. And my head seemingly vibrated with each stone I touched as well. From the level of headache pain I was experiencing I was surprised that I was not bleeding from my eyeballs.

"Which one is the Hierophant?" I asked, barely managing to keep my eyes open.

"He's the one enthroned between two pillars," Girolamo said as he pointed to the proper image. "Then the Moon, the Devil, Death, and Strength." He quickly pointed to each image I was supposed to paw at—as he studied my movements.

"Does this hurt?" he asked.

"Yes," I answered, giving him a fake smile.

Which he couldn't see anyway from behind my mask. So that was a bit pointless.

When I touched the final stone and all six of the images were glowing, the wall behind the fountain began to make creaking sounds.

The fountain and the wall split in two and slowly moved apart. Through the opening that formed I saw a large room full of beautiful objects.

It was a wonderful feeling—finding something so hidden, mysterious—and valuable. It could easily become addicting. No wonder treasure-hunters are such freaks.

"Yes!" Girolamo shouted.

I looked over at Tiziano, expecting him to be just as excited. But he stood as still as a statue and said nothing. He just kept staring at me.

Once the wall had parted enough for us to fit through, we scurried into the next room.

There were works of art everywhere. Paintings, tapestries, vases, sculptures.

"It's not here," Girolamo said to Tiziano, who didn't reply. As he was too busy staring at me.

How could he tell so quickly? The room itself was the size of my whole house, and it would've taken weeks to search it for one painting or statue. But it was obvious where Uri-dee-cee was located.

Apollo had immediately scampered over to a marble sculpture of a (naked) woman who was caught in flames as a hand reached up from the ground to grab hers.

It wasn't a comforting image.

She was clearly being pulled back to a place she didn't want to go to.

I walked toward her—wanting to bring her to life so she could cast off that hand and leave those flames.

But Tiziano grabbed my arm roughly before I could join Apollo.

"Wait," he said in a different tone than he had used before. "You're coming with me."

"What are you doing?" Girolamo asked him.

"I'm taking her with me," Tiziano said.

"You're doing what?" Girolamo asked.

Tiziano now had a death-grip on my right arm.

"Oh, no. No, no, no," Apollo said. "No, dear me. No. You aren't taking her anywhere. She's *my* lejer-demani. I found her first and I call dibs. Let her go."

"Perhaps not," Tiziano said coldly.

Apollo strode across the room in a flash and swiftly punched Tiziano across the face.

The sound was like fresh celery crunching between your teeth.

Tiziano dropped to the ground.

He moaned in pain and clutched at his face.

"*What was that?!?!?*" Girolamo asked Apollo, shocked.

Apollo dropped the outfit he had been carrying

for Eurydice. Then he took off his mask, hat, and cloak, also dropping them to the floor.

He glared at Girolamo as he stood there nearly buck-naked.

"If you can't tell—I'm a god made of solid marble, and I just broke your friend's jaw. Feel free to try me if you want something shattered, too," he said.

"Ah. That makes more sense now. You're a statue of a *god*," Girolamo said, nodding.

An *AWESOME* statue of a god.

Like a really effing awesome, naked statue who breaks people's jaws.

I have to admit—I was impressed.

Girolamo took off his mask and looked at Apollo.

"I'm no danger to you, friend," Girolamo said and sighed, looking down at Tiziano writhing in pain.

"Ah—I see," Apollo answered.

What did he see?

I saw that Girolamo was super-good-looking.

"Why are you so hot?!" I asked him.

Like clearly and totally hot. Like supermodel hot. Like a discomforting level of hotness. The kind that makes you blurt out stupid questions like a moron.

He looked at me, and it dawned on him that he had just taken his mask off. And I could see him—like 100%.

"He's a more complex individual than I initially gave him credit for," Apollo huffed and scowled at him.

"I'm…" Girolamo began, but just then the sound of several voices drifted up from the library.

They were loud and sounded angry.

"Guards. Or agents," Girolamo said as he put his mask back on. "You guys should get out of here."

"Come on Stella—let's wake up Eurydice," Apollo said.

"But what about them?" I asked.

"After whatever Tiziano wanted to do, they're on their own," Apollo replied.

"We'll be fine," Girolamo said as he helped Tiziano to his feet, and dragged him out the doorway. "I'll close this behind us so they can't come in here."

And with that—they were gone.

The stone walls started moving back together.

I took off my disguise and walked over to Eurydice. As I held Apollo's hand, I touched hers as well. I studied her carved face, her stone hair, and

I thought about how much Apollo loved her. So much so that he basically tricked/kidnapped me to come and get her. A song came into my head and I began to hum it.

I also thought about Girolamo and Tiziano, and what would happen to them.

Would they be caught by the guards and arrested?

I tried to push that out of my mind.

Not my problem.

Hum.

Hum.

Hum.

Not my problem.

"Wonderful!" Apollo said gleefully.

I opened my eyes and Eurydice was there before me, blinking and squeezing my hand. Apollo helped her off the pedestal. The hand reaching out from the base of the sculpture grabbed for her feverishly, but Apollo had already helped free her.

"Thank you," she said to me.

"No problem."

"Are you surprised to see me!?" Apollo asked and then sighed lovingly as he gazed into her face.

"I thought you'd find me somehow," she answered as she coyly pushed her hair behind her ear.

"Okay, let's go home," I said. "Those guards might know how to open that door."

"I doubt it. But still, we should go," Apollo said.

We stood in a circle, holding hands like hippies at a peace rally.

"Remember, think about me and I can lend you my strength," Apollo said.

Right. Apollo. God of the sun, of prophecy, of breaking people's jaws when they threaten to kidnap me from my kidnapper, of marble, nakedness, and love.

His song came into my head.

I hummed it—although I wanted to sing it. Shout it from the rooftops. But I didn't know if it had any words. Maybe they were just: 'Home, home, home!'

I closed my eyes and concentrated....

"NO TOUCHING!!!"

My eyes flew open and they met those of the museum guard who had just yelled at me. I instinctively let go of Apollo and Eurydice's hands.

"Sorry," I said.

I stepped back from them and looked up.

There they were—perched on pedestals. Holding hands.

But motionless.

I looked into Apollo's face, but he didn't look back.

Were they no longer 'alive?'

Or were they just pretending to be statues?

"Pssssttt," I said to them.

But they didn't reply.

I made some hand gestures toward their faces, but the only one looking at me was the guard. In fact—he was glaring at me.

I moved away and sat down on a bench.

I could do the humming thing again. Bring them back. But then what? We would walk out of the museum arm in arm?

The guards would pummel me first.

I glanced back at the two statues.

Even though they weren't moving anymore, they looked happy. That's what was important. Apollo had found Eurydice. They were together now, and I was back in Cali-fornia.

I was sighing heavily on the bench when I saw a cat walk by the doorway to the next gallery.

In the museum.

Inside the museum.

A cat.

Inside the museum.

Walking around on two feet. Wearing a back-pack.

Once again, I looked around to see if anyone else was seeing what I was seeing. But no one seemed to notice the cat. Clearly, my hallucination was continuing.

My hallucination? Had it been one?

Then I remembered the marble powder that Apollo had blown in my face. I scratched my head feverishly and then looked at my fingers. There it was. If the presence of an Eurydice sculpture in a place where there had not previously been an Eurydice sculpture wasn't enough proof for me, the dust was.

The cat walked by the doorway again.

And then he walked into the gallery I was in.

And stared right at me.

And sighed.

"Hello, Stella," he said. "I've been looking for you."

CHAPTER EIGHT.

Continuing What Happens to Poor Pathetic Stella.

As Presented by Poor Pathetic Stella.

"Hello, Stella," the cat said. "I've been looking for you. We've got to get out of here. We have to get as far away from this museum as possible."

"What are you talking about? And why is a cat talking to me???"

"There's no time! Run!"

(Stella: Okay, Maple? If you thought I was running in this story—you are seriously mistaken. I'm not running. I don't run. That's written in my contract. No running.

And did you really think I was going to grab this cat and run out of a maximum security art museum where if anybody is caught running they'll probably be tackled by like 50 guards in half a minute for fear that you are trying to steal art or run away after you peed on something?

Also, even if we run—the only way off this hill is on that darn tram, so we'd pretty much just be running like idiots to go wait in line at the tram.

Maple: You have brought up some interesting points. Cough.)

~~"There's no time! Run!"~~

"Whatcha doin'?" my father asked casually as he sat down next to me on the bench.

#thanksphonegpstracker

Now I understood why he had given me that super fancy phone for 'back to school stuff' this year—so that he could stalk me more efficiently.

I looked at my father.

My father looked at me.

I looked at the cat.

The cat looked at my father.

But my father didn't look at the cat.

"Um. Hi. Dad. You don't see that?" I asked, pointing to the cat.

"See what?"

"He can't see me. His powers have been locked away, somehow. In a weird way. I can't tell how," the cat replied, squinting at my father. "I can just tell that he once had them—but doesn't right now."

"There's a talking cat standing right here," I told my father, continuing to point at said cat.

"We have to go," my father said, standing up quickly.

"Okay...."

And he grabbed my hand and we *walked briskly* out of the museum.

(Note: We didn't run. Note: Don't run in museums kids. Note: Also, don't run in museums adults. Note: Nobody should be running in museums.)

Then we waited in line for the tram.

As we boarded it to go back down the hill, my father asked, "Is the cat still with us?"—with obvious panic in his voice.

Yes, the cat was still with us.

In fact, he was sitting on his tiny furry butt right next to me on the tram.

Like a tiny furry person with a tiny furry butt.

But my father seemed to be freaking out so much, I decided not to tell him.

"No," I lied. "It didn't follow us."

The cat nodded his head, apparently agreeing

with my decision to lie.

"*What's going on here?!*" my father and I asked each other simultaneously.

"I'm talking first here," my father insisted. "You have a lot of explaining to do, young lady. Why were you at the museum by yourself?! I told you to *never* do that."

"Ummmm."

Do I counter with: 'Why didn't you ever tell me I had bizarre arty magical powers, Dad?'

Probably not. That will only aggravate him more.

I looked at the cat—who shrugged.

"*And???*" my father pushed. "There's more to this than 'um.'"

"Well, let's be honest here, right?" I said, as a sort of half-suggestion-half-question.

"Yes, honesty is a good start."

"So I saw Mom's ghost and she told me to come here."

"You what? *She what?!*"

"It's just as I said. You remember how I had that nightmare on the morning of Halloween? Well, when I woke up, Mom's ghost was in my bedroom, talking to me. And then she vanished. And then she reappeared this morning in the bathroom and wrote on the mirror to come here. I thought she'd meet me here, so I came. Even though I wasn't supposed to. And she did meet me here, and she taught me how to hum songs to activate statues, and then she vanished."

"What on—what?" he asked.

"That's sort of where I'm at as well," I replied.

"And the cat?"

"Uh, the cat showed up right after I came back from Venice with the statue of Apollo, and then he started talking to me."

"*You went to Venice with a statue?!*" his voice was definitely getting angrier.

But he was trying very hard to hide it.

And yet I could tell that once we got in our car—away from all these lovely, innocent people on the tram—he was going to lose it.

"I *did* go to Venice with a statue. But I didn't mean to. I mean, I didn't know what I was doing. I didn't know what would happen."

"Your mother's ghost didn't tell you what would happen? She didn't tell you to go to Venice?"

"No, she just told me to think about the statue and start humming. Then she was gone."

He furrowed his brow and sat there quietly until

the tram reached the bottom of the hill.

Then the three of us walked to the car—in silence.

And the three of us got into the car—in silence.

The cat jumped into the passenger's seat, and then into the back seat. He sat there like a toddler we had just picked up from preschool, waiting patiently for his snack and juice box. He noticed me staring at him.

"Don't pay too much attention to me or your father will wonder what you're looking at," he said.

I looked away, settled myself into the passenger's seat, and stared out the windshield like my life depended on it.

"What was the nightmare about?" my father finally spoke again.

"Well, I was walking down a road and I found a gate. And I wanted to go through it, but I couldn't. And then a weird man showed up."

"What kind of weird man?"

"A man who wasn't one. He was really just a skeleton, wearing a mask."

My father's face turned pale and serious.

"What was this man doing?" he asked.

"Well, he told me to come with him. But

then...."

"Yes?"

"He started to strangle me," I said.

"Ah."

And then my father went quiet again.

And then I realized something.

I had gone insane.

I had literally gone insane.

Skeleton men. Ghosts of dead mothers. Time-traveling statues. Talking cats.

Sure, there was marble dust in my hair. But what did that prove? I could be imagining that in my totes messed up brain.

"Dad, you have to tell me something. Like don't lie. Do you see marble dust on my hand?"

"Yes."

"And it's in my hair?"

"Yes, yes it is. Clearly we need you to shower once we get home. Why are you asking me if it's there?"

"Well, if it's there, then I'm not crazy. I didn't imagine it if you see it, too."

"You're not crazy. You didn't imagine any of this."

I didn't?

Why was he so sure?

Clearly, he knew about all of this stuff and he just hadn't told me.

"I thought for sure you'd want to commit me by now—*why aren't you surprised by any of this?*" I asked.

"Because—well, I suppose it was only a matter of time. I was hoping I would never have to explain any of this to you. But apparently my plan didn't work out. Which is rather disappointing, on many levels."

"Vague, much?" I replied.

"Yes, well...."

"Tell him that the talking cat told you that you have to get as far away from that Apollo statue as possible. Tell him about how Tiziano tried to kidnap you in Venice, so it's too dangerous to stay here," the cat said.

How did this feline know about all of that???

"Go on tell him, we can't be sitting here all night!" the cat said.

So I explained what the cat told me to explain. And it all sounded really, really stupid and awkward coming out of my mouth. And it was at that moment that I decided that oral-folk-tale-teller was not going to be something I should pursue as a career.

"Tiziano? That was his name?" my father asked.

"Yes...."

"Then we leave L.A. tonight," he replied.

"*We what????*" I gasped.

"We fly to Connecticut tonight. When we get home, shower all of that marble dust off of you. All of it. Scrub everything off. Shower three times if you have to.

"And then pack for a long trip. Bring your cold weather clothes and anything valuable. Your laptop. Keepsakes, etc. Don't bring any of your school stuff though. We don't need that. Just the important stuff. We're basically going to have to move there until I figure out a plan."

"*We what?!?!?!?*" I gasped again.

The three of us drove home from the art museum.

Well, my father drove the car. I just sat there. Wondering what the heck to do about that talking cat in the backseat.

And wondering why we suddenly had to move to Connecticut, overnight.

But my father, in classic-Dad-fashion, sternly told me, "We'll talk about it later."

And I couldn't spend the ride home talking to the talking cat, getting answers to my questions from him, because then my father would know he was in the car.

So I just sat there—twitching.

Back at home I went into the bathroom to shower 626 times to get the marble dust out of my hair, and the cat joined me.

Awkward.

"I apologize for coming into the bathroom with you, but it's probably the only place where we can talk and your father won't hear us. I'm coming to Connecticut with you, but don't tell your father. We'll deal with all of that when we get to wherever we're going."

"Do you know where we're going? Mystery-talking-cat-thingy?"

"Oh, right. My name's Archie," he said as he held out his paw to shake my hand.

(Stella: *Hold on! Wait, wait, wait.* Maple? Maple— are you there? Answer me you pain in the butt.

Maple: Yes? What do you want?

Stella: You said before that Archie is my love interest.

Maple: Yes, yes he is.

Stella: He's a *cat.*

Maple: Yes, yes he is.

Stella: *I'm going to be in love with a cat???*

Maple: Yes, yes you are. Kind of.

Stella: Um, can I demand a rewrite?!?!

Maple: No, no you can't.

Stella: Look. I don't know what kind of sick, twisted thing you're writing here—but I can't be in love with a cat. That's insane.

Maple: Yes, yes it is insane.

Stella: If I have to be in love with someone for this stupid story—don't make him a cat! Make it a human being!

Maple: Yes, yes you have to be in love with someone for this stupid story.

Stella: This is going nowhere. Are you even paying attention to what I'm saying?!?!

Maple: No, no I'm not.

Stella: Son of a....

Maple: And now back to our previously scheduled programming, folks!!!)

"Oh, right. My name's Archie," he said as he held out his paw to shake my hand.

So I shook his tiny paw.

(Stella: *HIS PAW BECAUSE HE'S A BLASTED CAT!!!!!*

Maple: Ssssshhhhhhh.)

"Well, you already seem to know my name is Stella."

"Yes. But as far as your question, I don't know where we're going in Connecticut. As long as it's far away from that Apollo statue, it works for me."

"So Tiziano still wants to kidnap me or kill me or something—even though he was like in—1781? How does that make sense?"

"Well, because Tiziano time-traveled to 1781 Venice, just like you did."

"Through a statue?"

"No, not through a statue. But he did come from a different time."

"What time was that?"

"Um, I'm not sure exactly—but not the time that you came from."

"Is it okay if I'm totally confused?"

"I suppose so...."

"And who exactly are you? Where do you fit into these events?"

"I...."

"You okay in there???" my father asked through the bathroom door after he knocked on it.

"Uh, yeah, yeah. I was just—uh—reading memes

175

aloud."

Lamest. Answer. Ever.

And totally obvious.

"Don't come in—I'm naked," I added for good measure.

"Um. Okay—but take a shower, stat," he yelled. "Stop goofing off! But let me know if you feel sick or anything weird happens in there. But take a shower right now."

Yes.

Like I was goofing off.

I was talking to a cat trying to figure out the mysteries of the universe here, Dad.

All the mysteries that you already seem to know, but won't tell me about, *Dad*.

"Okay!" I answered him.

And then I whispered, "We'll talk more after I shower—Archie."

The cat nodded, jumped up onto the sink, and sat down on the counter with his little legs hanging off it. Then he adorably covered his eyes with his paws and said, "You can get undressed now."

As I carefully took off my clothes, I studied him —partly to make sure he was keeping his eyes covered and partly out of pure curiosity.

He was a large grey tabby. With five fingers on his

front paw-leg thingies—like tiny little furry hands with opposable thumbs. Polydactyl or Pterodactyl. Or something like that. Some weird big word from the 'p' section of the dictionary that I can't quite remember for sure.

Also he had this delicate tan belly-fur-fluff that was all out there in the open because he was sitting on his butt like a person. And all I wanted to do was molest that fluff. But I resisted the urge.

Then I heard my father talking.

I think on the phone.

Hopefully not to himself, nor to another talking cat. I don't think I can handle more than one of those at a time.

No, it definitely sounded like my father's phone voice. You know how people get a different voice when they're talking on the phone? Like are you trying to pretend you're someone else? Or you just want to sound like a TV announcer to the people on the other end of the line?

Well, anyway, my father was using his phone voice, and I think I heard him say the words 'penny' and 'bad girls would.'

CHAPTER NINE.

Returning To Morrow's World in 'Bad Girls Would,' aka Badger's Wood.

By Morrow.

(Morrow: I told you to stop putting the word 'to' in front of my darn name, Maple.

Maple: To Morrow, To Morrow, I Love….

Morrow: Shut up, you craven, ill-bred, onion-eyed….

Maple: Ah. *Yes.* I hear it—the subtle sounds of a character who wants to be gruesomely beheaded in this next section….

Morrow: Uh, forget I said that. Where was I again in this tale? Oh, yes….)

I woke up to the sound of hushed voices and two figures moving around in the darkness in our bedroom.

They fumbled with a flashlight near the bookcases.

"The notebook should be around here some-where. I know I shoved it behind the books on this shelf so no one would be able to find it," Nora whispered.

She was obviously Shadowy Figure #1.

"Well, I don't see any notebook in here," Ellie whispered back.

Shadowy Figure #2.

I leaned out of my bed and flipped on my night-stand lamp.

"What notebook are you guys talking about?" I asked.

"*Sssshshhhh*," they responded simultaneously.

"Penny will hear you," Nora said. "Or even worse, Eagle. He has ears like—like, well—he has really good ears."

"He's already heard you," I explained. "He hears everything that goes on in this house, and hon-estly, people in China could probably hear you. You aren't as quiet as you think you are. What notebook are you guys talking about?"

"Um, the notebook where I wrote down some ideas for a 'how to make a man' spell," Nora said as she winked at me.

"You wrote down—huh?" I asked. "Wait, what's

going on? Am I still asleep or did you just say that you have a spell for making a *man*?"

"Yes, Norad and I were going to try and see if we could, ya know, make a man," Ellie said, also winking at me.

Was this some sort of a symbiotic facial tic they had recently developed?

"We only do the spells Eagle teaches us, you numbskulls," I replied. "And never in the house. What are you guys trying to accomplish exactly?"

"A notebook with what?" Eagle asked from the doorway. "Accomplish what?"

"*Dog balls*," Nora said and sighed. "He caught us."

"What exactly did I catch you three doing?" Eagle continued.

"Well, we were going to do a little extracurricular magic here in our room, while you weren't watching. And make a man," Ellie explained to him, with a faux innocent tone to her voice.

Was she insane? Why was she telling him this? Shouldn't she be telling him a lie??? What was she trying to do? Get us all killed?

"And the point of that would *be*???" I asked, completely flustered. "To what? Get us in trouble with Penny? To let her know that we've been studying and practicing magic for several months now?

Would that be the point of that?!?"

"Well, clearly Morrow didn't know what you two pignuts were up to," Eagle said as he blinked at Nora and Ellie. "So you'll have to explain to both of us what the point of making a man would be."

"The point would be to *make a man*, which you kept refusing to let me do," Ellie whined. "Norad and I are almost teenagers and we've never even *seen* a boy before. I mean they're like—half of our species! Do you think that's fair??"

"Do I think it's fair that they're half the species?" Eagle asked. "Well, I guess I've never really thought about that before. Should they be? Should they only be a third of the species? But you do still need them to reproduce, ya know? Well, you kind of need them to reproduce—well, I'm not going to explain this to you three. Anyway —y'all have seen a boy before. If your father can count as a boy, you definitely saw him. And some other male humanesque people as well."

"It's just that none of us can *remember* seeing them because we were all basically babies when we came here," Nora said. "So it's like we've never seen them. You see? So we want to see what one looks like."

"Wait," I interrupted. "Ellie wants to see a boy? I highly doubt it. She's too busy looking at herself to look at someone else. Even if they are an exotic male of the species."

"I didn't really care too much about seeing a boy, one way or another. I just wanted to see if we could do the spell successfully," Ellie responded. "It does seem like a challenging one."

Nora glared at her in response.

"Well, maybe I wanted to see a man," Ellie admitted. "A little bit."

"Curiosity killed the cat," Eagle interjected. "Thank goodness I interrupted whatever insanity you had planned. There's no magic outside of our sessions, so now go back to bed. I'll spend the next few hours coming up with ways to punish y'alls."

Nora and Ellie looked at me.

It was the 'we've got a plan so play along' look.

I guess that was what all the winking had been about.

Why hadn't they just let me in on the plan from the beginning??? Stupid pignuts.

Nora began to fake-cry, and Ellie patted her on the back with fake-sympathy.

"You *never* let us do anything we want to do. *Man*, I had already started thinking up names for him," Nora sniffled. "Gustaf. No, Logan. Wait, maybe Finn…."

"Names? *Really!?* This was your worst idea *ever*," Eagle said. "Shut up and go to sleep, you idiots."

"Why don't you want us to make a man?" I asked, hopefully playing into my sisters' plan.

"Because," he answered, a non-answer.

"Why don't you want us to *see* a man?" Ellie asked, going in a different direction.

"Because," he answered, his favorite non-answer, again. "Well, it's not like I don't want you to *see* a man. I just don't want you guys to do the spell to *make a man*. Duh. See the difference?"

"Well, *you* could always *turn into a man*, so we could see one," Ellie suggested.

"I don't just shape-shift for hahas," he said, tsked and scowled at us.

"You've been a door, a duck, a chair. For no good reason. Let's see, you were that birthday cake once and you scared the life out of all of us. And there was that time you were a watering can, a tree, a rug, dish soap…" Nora said as she ticked items off on her fingers.

"Yeah, yeah, yeah," Eagle said and waved his arms dismissively at her.

"But you've never been *a man* before," Ellie

added.

"What do you guys need to see a man for? You have me right here!" Eagle said, jumping up and down. "I'm all the masculinity you need to see!"

"You're a rabbit, Eagle. You're fuzzy and cute. But you ain't a human man-like dude," I said matter-of-factly.

"I'm a springhare, dammit!!! *Not a rabbit!!!*"

"So you *can't become a man*," Ellie pushed. "That must be it. It's too complicated for you."

"I *can* become a man, too!!!" he explained haughtily. "I can do it! It's just the same as becoming anything else. No more or less complicated."

"Do it. Do it. Do it," Nora chanted, gently clapping in time with herself.

"*Who would want to become a human?* Not me," he scoffed. "Look at you, you hairless freaks. You need more fur. All that pink skin is disgusting. Might as well be a naked mole rat."

"It *is* probably too difficult for a springhare to turn into a full-grown man," I said slyly. "He just doesn't want to admit it to us."

"True," Ellie replied. "Too small."

"I'm not too small to turn into a man!" Eagle huffed. "I'm a powerful magical being, you turd-faced foot-lickers! I can turn into anything!"

"Well, anything that *Penny* tells you to turn into. I mean, she is in charge and all," Nora said, decisively nailing the coffin closed.

"*Whhhhaaaaaattttt?!?!?!*" Eagle shouted as loud as he could. "Ugghhhh! Penny isn't in charge! I'm in charge! Look at me! I'm in charge and I can do anything! You want a man! Fine, I'll give you a man!"

Sometimes his hot-blooded temper was useful.

So Eagle scrunched his face into the 'I'm constipated' look we had seen on him so many times before. His little face turned pinkish as he held his breath. And then two clouds of white pigmenty smoke shot out of his paws and enveloped him. And within this cloud his tiny springhare body transformed into a man.

A human man. Full-grown.

Like six feet tall. Brown hair. Tan. Blue eyes. Sculpted body.

And naked. Well, Eagle hadn't been wearing any clothes.

He was a springhare after all.

Nora stared at him with a look of sheer horrified —but still curious—terror. Her quiet clapping had stopped abruptly.

Ellie's mouth dropped open and I would say her expression was one of marked inquisitiveness.

I tried to look away and stare at the ceiling. But it was like watching a train wreck. I couldn't avert my gaze.

Eagle was just standing there grinning. Naked as a jaybird. Hands on his hips. His naked, naked human man hips.

I had to admit...this *was* a special occasion.

None of us actually remembered seeing a man in the flesh. Sure we had seen them in pictures, on TV, on the Internet. But this was an entirely different experience.

Here was Eagle—as a living breathing man. He scratched his head. My eyes followed the movement, just like my sisters' eyes. We were all entranced.

I kinda wanted to touch him.

But I wasn't the first one with that thought. Ellie was already moving forward with her arm outstretched toward his chest.

"What are you doing?" Eagle asked her.

He shifted his body away from her hand.

"What do you think I'm doing?" Ellie followed his movement and then made contact with her fingertips, right above where his heart was.

She stared up into his eyes.

Cough.

Who had coughed?

Was it a group-wide collective cough?

"You see, I told you I could do it," he said, staring back at her, but stepping away.

This was Eagle the springhare—but yet it *sooooo* wasn't.

"I have no idea what's going on here, but at least cover yourself up, Eagle," Penny said as she appeared in the doorway half-asleep, pajamas disheveled, hair a mess, and glasses barely hanging onto her face.

She tossed Eagle a pillow from a nearby chair.

He caught it. Looked down at himself and then held the pillow in front of him. A shy smile came across his face.

A look I had never seen before.

Not on Eagle.

Not on anyone.

He backed slowly out of the room, pillow firmly in place. He scooted past Penny and then ran down the hallway. I could hear the heavy tromping of his human feet.

Eagle self-conscious.

Eagle was self-conscious.

I had never seen him like that. He wasn't a shy type of rabbit. He was a bold, confident pain in the butt.

Whoever that was, wasn't Eagle.

Or was it just a side of him we had never seen before?

Penny continued to stand in the doorway, limp like a zombie, with her eyes closed, breathing deeply as if she was falling back asleep.

"They tricked me!" Eagle shouted from down the hallway. "They wanted to know what a man looked like. They tricked me! It's their fault!"

"What?" Penny asked as she cocked her head and raised both eyebrows. Her eyes were still closed though.

"It was Norad's idea," Ellie said, trying to save her own butt.

So much for sisterly loyalty.

"It was not *just* my idea. You wanted to see a man, too," Nora replied.

"I don't care whose idea it was," Penny said and yawned. "Rule Number Two: Don't aggravate or trick Eagle. He'll only end up making us all pay. Also, I'm not sure I should be telling you this right now, but I'm still mostly asleep so my sense of judgment is grossly diminished."

"What? What shouldn't you be telling us?" Nora prodded.

"You'll get to see a real human man. Soon," she said. "Like tomorrow-ish. And not one who is actually a springhare shadow creature. This one is more realistically proportioned and not built like an underwear model."

What was she talking about?

"Why can't it be an underwear model?" Ellie asked, missing the larger issue.

"Why? Because it's Derek, and Derek is not an underwear model. That's why. He is coming here and bringing Stella with him. So they will be living with us from now on. He called earlier from L.A. to tell me that they are flying here right now."

This was huge news.

"*This is HUUUUUGGGGEEEE news!*" Nora squealed at the top of her lungs.

It was a noise that could shatter glass.

"You're kidding, right? People are coming here?" I asked. "That never happens. Is this a joke? Are you kidding?"

"Nope, not kidding. Stella's powers are coming into play now, unfortunately. So they've got to come here to be safe and figure out well, that's not important right now," Penny said as she finally opened one eye. "This means that you all have to be mature and nice. And don't—*absolutely don't*—

189

expect Derek to stand naked in front of you like Eagle just did. Normal human men don't do that.

"So be nice. Did I say that already? Don't cause trouble. These are our guests, our friends. We don't really have any of those, so let's treasure our new friends and not be—uh, annoying to them. Gosh, I'm tired. Are you guys insane? It's like 4 am. You guys are *sooo* gonna get it when I'm awake. And not even for that tricking Eagle stuff. But for waking me up."

Then Penny opened both her eyes, widened them, turned her mouth into a snarl, and sliced her hand across her throat, threateningly—all while growling like a wild animal. Afterward, she shuffled away like the half-asleep zombie she was.

I remained sitting up in bed while Nora and Ellie stood very still by the bookshelf.

All three of us were waiting to hear Penny's bedroom door close down the hallway. The noise finally came, and we let out a joint sigh of relief.

"Maybe she'll forget what happened by the time she wakes up," Nora said.

Fat chance.

"*Oh my gosh!* Did you see him? Did you see him?" Ellie was now literally jumping up and down.

I think she might start an earthquake.

"Did I see who?" I asked. "Dude, calm down. That was just Eagle. I think you're missing the more mind-numbingly amazing issue at hand of people actually coming here to live with us."

"That wasn't Eagle," Ellie gasped. "That was someone else. That was like a *god! A dream! A dream man!*"

She had evidently lost the cool that she had been trying so hard to maintain all these past years. Maybe she was really a boy-obsessed tween at heart? God. That would be horrific.

"I have to admit, that was something else there. I mean—*dang*," Nora said and nodded, agreeing to a discussion that seemed to mostly be going on in her own head.

It was difficult to avoid thinking about that moment. That moment that was completely uncomfortable and simultaneously thrilling. That moment that infamously became known amongst the three of us as simply: 'The MacGuffin.'

I shook my head to clear the image from my mind.

"Okay, all that skin and stuff aside," I said and then coughed. "Stella and this Derek guy...."

"What do you guys think Derek looks like?" Ellie interrupted. "How old do you think he is? Too bad

Stella isn't a boy. Do you think anybody else is going to move here to live with us? Maybe a family with a teenage son? But not one we're related to. Are we related to Derek? But then again, he's old—right?"

Nora and I exchanged a glance—both our faces stricken with fear.

We had unwittingly created a monster.

CHAPTER TEN.

The Most Exciting Day of Our Lives.

By Morrow.

Derek and Stella arrived when we were in the kitchen, making what felt like the hundredth type of cannoli for Eagle. Who was dancing on the kitchen table and singing "*La donna è mobile*" at the top of his lungs.

We all heard a chime.

A type of chime noise we'd never heard before.

"What was that?" Nora asked.

Penny came out of the library and stared at us all for a moment.

"What are you guys doing?" she asked.

"Making cannoli," Nora answered.

"It seems like you guys have been making an awful lot of desserts this year..." Penny's voice trailed off.

"We started a baking club back in April," Ellie explained. "Didn't we tell you?"

"Ah," Penny said and eyed us suspiciously.

"Ya know—to learn more about world cuisine," Nora added.

"Right," she agreed, clearly knowing we were lying.

She looked at Eagle.

"What?" he asked.

"Nothing, for now. Well, they're here. Let's go out to the front yard and let them in," Penny said.

"*What?!?!?!?*" Nora squealed.

"That noise!" Ellie gasped. "That chime meant they're here!"

So we all piled out the front door of our cottage like the Queen of England had arrived.

But nobody was out there.

"*Where are they???*" Nora whined.

"We still have to let them in," Penny said.

A black iron letterbox started to rise up out of a grassy patch in the front yard. We had never seen this thing before. What did it do???

"What's that???" Nora asked as she went to go touch it.

"Nora, no touching, please," Penny said as she opened the little letterbox's door, which had a horse and rider on it, dashing off to somewhere to make a delivery.

Inside was a red envelope. Penny took it out, opened it up, and read what was written on a small piece of paper inside it. (But not out loud, why not??? Why do we have to be perpetually left in the dark???)

Then she said something under her breath, put the piece of paper back into the envelope, put the envelope back into the letterbox, and closed the door.

"I don't know what you just did but I've never been so excited in my life," Nora said as she squirmed with anticipation.

"If you were a dog, your tail would be wagging off its hinges," Eagle grumbled. "Lower your expectations, Norad. You people have no idea what excitement really is."

I nodded in agreement with him, trying to get some perspective on this situation and calm my own nerves. Despite my nodding, the rest of my body stood totally still, unsure of what to do with itself. And eventually I was unsure if I was even breathing.

Meanwhile Ellie tried to hide her trepidation, but she kept shifting her weight from one foot to the other every second.

Penny waved her hand across the yard, and the garden beds filled with blooming flowers, even though it was November. Even the air temperature seemed to be warmer than before. She was really rolling out the red carpet.

Eagle looked at her with a smug expression, and from his bum he shot a stream of rabbit-poo-balls across the sidewalk—which was now lined with blooming lavender irises and bluebells—as well as poop.

Penny rolled her eyes and with a wave of her hand the poop disappeared.

"You may find that in your bed later," she told him.

"Then you *may* have to clean it up later when I wipe my bed all over your bed," he said and then stuck his tongue out at her.

Then there was a sudden shift in the atmosphere, a vibration of the air.

Penny and Eagle looked at each other with furrowed brows.

"Was that Sven?" Nora asked.

"Sven?" Penny wondered. "Who's Sven?"

"That's what she's named the bubble force field thingy," I explained.

"Oh, right. Yes, it was Sven. But it was slightly odd."

"Well, if it was letting people in, it would shudder, right?" I asked.

"No," she answered. "No, that shouldn't have shifted the air like that."

Eagle was now scowling.

"You're in charge of this confounded thing, Penny-Poopy-Pants, can't you make it work properly?" he asked as he crossed his arms.

"Let's just greet our guests, and see what's going on then. I don't feel anymore changes in the air and the force field is still intact," she said.

Should we be worried?

"We'll be ready. For whatever that was, right?" Eagle looked at the three of us and nodded.

"Of course," Penny answered.

But he was really talking to us—the three Demington sisters—who secretly knew magic. He had been training us primarily in combat and defense spells, and little else. Hence, why he refused to let Nora make a man, which he deemed 'useless' for combat purposes. Which is kinda ironic if you think about how the history of human combat really boils down to men beating the poop out of each other, combatively.

I'm not sure if it was Eagle's combative attitude that drew him to fighting spells, but we knew it ultimately had something to do with our Aunt Verbena. That much was obvious.

"A car! I see a car!" Nora shouted.

"*Oooooo!*" Eagle mocked her. "*Do they still have cars in the real world?!? My god!*"

Indeed, there was a car. A big black SUV the size of our whole garage.

"I thought that there was just two of them?" Ellie asked, also surprised at the size of the mammoth vehicle.

"Well, I'm sure they have a lot of bags, Ellie. Remember they're going to be living with us now," Penny answered.

Oh yeah, right. They had to pack up their life in one evening. Their most important belongings reduced to luggage. Then they had to whisk their butts over here ASAP like fugitives on the run.

And here we were—a bunch of country bumpkins grinning from ear to ear at their arrival because we finally get to see a car and a man and new people after almost a decade. I felt kinda stupid. And a bit overwhelmed.

The SUV pulled into the driveway. A man—probably in his mid-40s—got out of the car. Black hair. Brown eyes. Tan skin. Tall-ish. Sort of muscular. He smiled and threw a little wave our way.

"He's so handsome," Ellie gasped under her breath.

"He's so ancient," Nora responded under hers.

"Shut up," I added under mine.

Then a girl got out of the passenger's seat. Also, tall-ish. Definitely taller than Penny. Black hair. Brown eyes. Tan-ish skin. Skinny as a rail.

"Phew—that was quite the trip!" Derek said to Penny as he gave her a quick hug.

"I'm just glad you were able to get here so fast," she responded. "I'm Penny. You must be Stella. I haven't seen you since you were a little, little girl."

"Yes, yes, that's me," the girl said, nodding.

My sisters and I—I am ashamed to admit—were standing there slack-jawed, wide-eyed, and silent. Like a bunch of Amish kids at a heavy metal concert.

"This is Eagle, Nora, Ellie, and Morrow," Penny said as she gestured to each of us in turn, and the Stella girl sheepishly smiled at us and gave a little wave.

My sisters and I remained expressionless dolts.

As Stella had gotten out of the car she left the car

door open, and just then a cat jumped down from the SUV.

He was walking like a human, like Eagle does.

Did that mean this cat was Derek's shadow creature?

"What? How?" Penny asked him. "*What are you doing here?!*"

"Uhhh-uh," Stella stuttered. "You can see him?"

"See who?!" Derek gasped. "*It's not that cat, is it? You told me he wasn't with us anymore!*"

"Well, I…" Stella started to answer him.

"It's the God of Destruction, Derek, calm down," Penny interrupted. "It's Archie, just as a cat."

"*Suntsitzea!?* What? Why is he with us???" Derek asked. "Is he dangerous?"

"I don't think so, though it would explain why the force field shuddered. If a god came into the bubble it would have a significant impact on the power structure of it," Penny commented, tapping her chin.

"Is it holding? Is the force field holding?!" Derek asked.

"Yes, yes. Don't worry about that," Penny answered him calmly.

"There are two reasons why your force field would shudder," Archie said. "First, yes, because I am the God of Destruction, sort of. And the second is because Stella is the next Jainkohiltzaile—the Godkiller—and she has a powerful aura. Similar to that of a god."

"Why is everyone quiet? Is the cat talking? What did the cat say?!?" Derek asked.

In an instant Derek was in full panic mode, throwing his hands up in the air, and muttering endlessly. Apparently he couldn't see or hear this cat guy Archie. And apparently the words 'calm' and 'collected' were not in his vocabulary.

"Great! This place is supposed to be safe, Penny," he continued. "You said it was safe here. And yet we have a cat-god following us in here! *What did he just say???*"

"It's okay, Derek. Everything is under control. Let me just figure this out with a simple conversation before you have an aneurysm," Penny told him.

"What's a Godkiller?" Stella asked Archie.

"You," Eagle replied as he sat down on the sidewalk with a stunned look on his face. "You. That's what this weird sensation is in my guts, huh? Stella is the *Jainkohiltzaile*."

"Godkiller? What?" Derek pushed. "What's going on?"

"Uh, Archie just said that Stella is the next God-killer," Penny told him as she scratched her head.

Derek then sat down on the sidewalk as well, with a stunned look on his face—just inches away from Eagle, whom he also apparently couldn't see —because he had almost sat on him.

"I'm sorry. I should have told you this when we met before," Archie said to Penny. "She's the next Jainkohiltzaile. Whatever you did to protect her worked and I thank you for that. But it seems as if something is blocking her full powers from coming to the surface and we need to unblock them. There's this God of Death we have to confront, and Stella needs to be able to do that."

"*A God of Death?!?*" Eagle gasped and then buried his face into his paws.

"Uh, well. I did that," Penny replied. "Well, Derek and I did that together. We cast a spell on her that would block her from becoming a lejerde-mani. Or at least, it was supposed to do that. Her powers were never supposed to manifest, ever."

"Ah, I see. That was your way to hide her. I get it. But as the Jainkohiltzaile her powers will manifest no matter what. And they will keep pushing against your spell like a battering ram against a locked gate. She is destined to be the Godkiller.

I'm afraid there is no lejerdemani spell that can prevent that from happening. So we need to take away your spell," Archie said.

"Is someone going to tell me what a Godkiller is?" Stella asked.

"You don't wanna know," Eagle said.

"I'll explain it to you later, honey," Derek said. "Will someone tell me what is happening?"

"Archie's saying that we need to release Pu. We need to take away the spell that we cast on Stella so that she can become the Godkiller without any further hindrance against her powers," Penny explained.

"But we can't do that!" Derek gasped.

"We have to do that," Archie answered.

"Archie's right," Penny said.

"What did the cat say?" Derek asked.

"*Oh god*! Can we just give this blasted man back Pu so we don't have to say everything *twice*!?!?!" Eagle shouted. "I'm going to pull my ears off having to listen to this painful game of telephone!"

"Yes. I think we should do that," Penny said. "We need to do that."

"Do what?!? What are we doing???" Derek asked.

"*Aaaaaaaaaaaaggghh!!! Aaaaaacccccckkkkkkk!!!!!!*" Eagle screamed as he kicked Derek across the face with his back leg.

Which was rather surprising for Derek, who didn't see it coming.

Literally.

"Stella, go to your room," Derek commanded once we had all piled back inside the house and he began applying a bag of frozen corn to his face.

"But, I don't even know where my room is," she responded, turning her hands in the air in an exasperated fashion.

"Derek, she's sixteen. I think it's probably time that she be allowed to listen to our conversations *about her*," Penny said and then sighed.

"I have something to talk about with you and Archie—wherever he is—that I don't want her to hear. Is that such a crime? *I am her father.*"

Penny and Derek glared at each other for several seconds, both clearly frustrated.

"Girls, can you please take Stella to your room?" Penny asked us as she rolled her eyes at Derek. "And stay there until we come and get you."

This was disappointing.

I wanted to stand in the kitchen and continue to listen to all this fascinating information that was pouring out of everyone's mouth.

"*Noooowwww*," Penny commanded when she noticed that the three of us weren't moving.

I sighed heavily. Nora whimpered a little. And Ellie motioned to Stella to follow us across the kitchen, through the foyer, down the hallway, and up the stairs.

"Do you think Eagle will tell us what they talk about?" Nora asked Ellie and me once we were securely in our bedroom, per Penny's instructions.

"I doubt it. But this situation is unprecedented, so you never know," I commented.

"I'll tell you what Eagle will tell you," Eagle said from the doorway as he entered the room and kicked the door closed behind him. "Everything that we've been doing was for lejerdemani vs. lejerdemani magical combat."

And then he kicked the poop out of the trash bin, flinging it up against the wall several times.

"*Stop that, Eagle!!!!!!*" Penny screamed up at him from the kitchen.

He growled in response.

"Why are you so angry?" Ellie asked him.

"When is he not angry?" I asked.

"I'm *extra* angry right now because all your skilzzzzzz are useless against a god," Eagle spat. "So if that God of Death shows up—or any other gods—hide. Use the most advanced camouflage spell I taught you. *And hide*."

"What?" I asked him. "We've been training like Navy Seals for months so that we can *hide*?!?!"

"Yes. At least you can do that. And hopefully it will work well enough that whatever god of the month it is that shows up will not notice you," he answered.

"But we're demi-gods," Nora said. "Well, half demi-gods, so like demi-demi-gods. Doesn't that count for anything?"

"No. God beats demi-god every time. It's like scissors versus paper. Scissors will always win," he warned.

"So what beats scissors?" Ellie asked. "What is the rock that can crush the scissors in this scenario?"

"She's the rock," Eagle pointed to Stella. "The Godkiller. The Jainkohiltzaile."

"Is this the part of the conversation where someone actually tells me what a Godkiller is?" Stella asked. "And that other word that you just said, what's a Jan-something?"

"Jainkohiltzaile is just 'Godkiller' in the old language. And the Godkiller kills gods, duh. That should be pretty obvious from the name," Eagle said as he rolled his eyes at her.

"I don't know how to do that," she said.

"Clearly. Clearly," Eagle said, nodding. "You'll have to be taught how to do that, just like any other Jainkohiltzaile."

"How many Godkillers are there?" she asked.

"Only one. There's some overlap during the end of one's lifetime over the lifetime of the next one, but basically only one at a time," Eagle replied. "But back to my main point. *Did you hear me, girls?* If anybody else shows up—*hide.*"

And with that order he left the room, slamming the door shut. And then he probably returned to the kitchen to participate in that fascinating conversation we were missing out on.

"Are you guys really good at hiding?" Stella asked.

"I can see where you're probably going with this," Ellie responded. "But each of us only knows how to cast a spell to hide ourselves. That way if one of us is caught, only one of us is caught—get it? It's limiting. But we've only learned what Eagle felt like teaching us. Which Penny doesn't know about at all. So we're kind of—limited."

"Ah. So you can't hide me, too? Not even from my Dad?" Stella said and then fake-laughed. "He's so mad that I brought the cat with us. Well, Archie.

Archie the cat-god thingy. Oh, what's this?"

And then she was gone.

Stella had absentmindedly picked up a die from the floor that was next to her foot.

And then she had disappeared.

"*Oh. My. God!*" Ellie's screaming voice quivered and then she sucked in her breath.

"*What just happened?!*" I asked my sisters in total and complete panic.

"She picked up one of my dice!" Nora cried. "I must have dropped it. But I always keep them in a bag in my nightstand!!!"

"*What are you talking about?!*" Ellie pleaded with her.

Nora scrambled over to her nightstand, which Stella had been next to, and discovered that the top drawer was partially open.

"There's a tiny robot in here!" she gasped.

And indeed there was a tiny robot in the drawer. And he had opened a bag of dice and was throwing them out of the drawer onto the floor.

"Those eight-sided dice that were in Horace's study!!!" Ellie yelled as she slapped Nora across the back. "*Why'd you take those?!?!*"

I grit my teeth and glared at Nora.

What had she done?

Where was Stella now???

"My bad," Nora said.

"*Why did you take them?!*" Ellie groaned, as she went to pick the other dice up from the floor to return them to the bag.

"No, don't," I stopped her. "What if they make you disappear, too?"

"They won't. They wouldn't," Nora shook her head. "I've been playing with them this whole time and they've never made me disappear like that!"

"*You've been playing with them this whole time?!?!*" Ellie repeated, nearly screaming again, but trying to keep her voice down.

"Only when I was in the bathroom. So no one would see. Why are you acting like I killed someone? I mean, *yeesh*. I only made a little game with them in my notebook to see how frequently I would roll certain numbers," Nora said, squirming. "It's not like I was practicing dark, evil magic with them."

"Clearly they are magical, Nora. They just *deleted* Stella from this room," I said and then sighed.

"What's going on in here?" Penny asked as she burst into the room.

"Uhhhhhhh," Nora answered.

So we had to explain what happened, and why it happened. Well, as much as we understood anyway.

Penny's face went from horror to dismay back to horror to shock to disappointment then to anger, and finally settled on something like panicked determination.

Derek skipped over all of the stuff where we broke the rules about going into Horace's study and got to the heart of the matter, "Where did she go?! Where is my daughter?!"

We all looked at each other, waiting for an intelligent answer from somebody.

"I have no idea," Penny said and sighed. "Those dice are not transport devices."

"What if they are, and we just didn't know it?" Derek asked. "How do we get her back?"

"If they are—if it's possible—if she stops touching the die, the transport state will cease," Penny explained.

"But how do we get her to stop touching it?" Ellie asked.

"We don't," Penny answered. "She's got to do that herself."

CHAPTER ELEVEN.

In Which I Find Myself in a Nasty Place.

By Stella.

The instant I picked up the die from the floor I found myself in a cavernous dump.

The nice comfortable bedroom full of squishy beds and overstuffed chairs and lovely overflowing bookcases in the idyllic country cottage was gone.

Layers of old striped wallpaper hung off the walls of this decaying room. Chunks of wood and plaster were all over the floor. Dust crept into my nostrils and throat, and I began to cough and hack. Nice. Just what I needed.

I looked for a window to get some fresh air and saw one at the far end of the room.

As I began to walk toward it I felt eyes watching me from somewhere.

The wallpaper pieces shifted somewhat in a breeze that I could not feel.

I stopped moving forward. And listened instead.

The wall closest to me creaked.

I stared at it.

Slowly, a pair of eyes grew out of the wall, looking at me.

My gut hardened.

What was I supposed to do now?

A figure walked up from behind me, approached the wall, and violently gouged those two wall eyes out with its fingers.

The creature in the wall screamed. Dark blood ran down the wall. I looked away and tried not to throw up.

And then the figure turned to me.

Where did he—or it—come from?

I hadn't even sensed that he was next to me.

His head was like an enormous bird skull that had been covered with old, wrinkled leather. Two eyes protruded from the top of the skull. Solid black. The size of billiard balls. I could tell he was looking at me despite his lack of pupils. His mouth opened up slowly. It was a cross between a beak and a crocodile's jaws. His gnarled, rotting teeth were revealed, and the corners of the mouth curled up in a smile.

"Hewantedtoeatyou," the creature said to me in a horrid hiss. It came out as one gurgled, mucus-coated word. "ButIwanttoeatyou."

Oh.

Shiiiii....

I took a step away from him as more of these monsters appeared in the wall. Their dark, spindly limbs oozed out of the wallpaper and reached for me. They began to step out of the wall, their legs covered in boney protrusions and pus-covered blisters.

What were these things?!?

They lunged toward me as I turned to run out of the room. The creatures followed.

They chased me down a hallway that led to another hallway.

They were gaining on me and every time I looked back, it seemed as if their muscles were growing, pushing outward in violent instantaneous bulges, making their arms and legs bigger and bigger, allowing them to run faster and faster.

I already told you, dear readers, that I don't run.

I'm not an athlete.

This was not going to be a long chase.

I ran to the end of a hallway, tripped into what seemed to be a walk-in closet, and locked the door behind me.

There were no other doors, and no windows.

This was a tattered, weary room like the one I had just been in. The only things in here were dust-covered broken wire hangers scattered on the cracked linoleum floor.

My breathing was heavy, panting.

My legs ached with pain.

'Why'd you have to run?!?!'—they pleaded with me.

Adrenaline filled my system. My head felt cloudy.

I listened intently for any sounds while I tried to stabilize my breathing.

My new friends—the nasty monsters—began to scrape against the door.

They were apparently trying their hardest to scratch the door to pieces.

It began to shake it on its hinges.

This was not a secure feeling.

Would the door hold?

I looked down at the die, still in my right hand.

"You little piece of crud, you brought me here now

take me away!" I yelled at it.

Wait....

I dropped the die onto the closet floor, and it hit the hardwood floor in the girls' bedroom, bounced off of it, and went onto a rug.

I looked up.

I had interrupted what seemed to be an interesting conversation between all the members of the household.

"She's apparently a lot smarter than she looks," Eagle said.

"That was—*simply terrifying*," I said, quickly looking around to check if any monsters had followed me.

Then I crawled onto the nearest bed, clutching its comforter.

"*Are you okay?! Are you okay?!*" my father asked as he ran over to me and started checking me over.

I guess to make sure that I was still his daughter and not an alien impostor.

"What happened???" Penny asked.

After I caught my breath, I told them where I had gone to, and about the wallpaper monsters, and about how I should probably change my underwear because of the possible urine and poo stains.

Okay, I didn't say that last part out loud.

I just thought it.

"You said striped wallpaper? And monster things with birdlike heads?" Penny asked.

"Yeah," I replied.

"That was probably my childhood home in Pipistrelle Village," she said.

"*What?!?!?*" my father shouted. "This is exactly the thing I wanted to avoid! What do you mean that was *probably* your house?!?!?"

"My Mom loved striped wallpaper. She put it up in the living room, remember?" Penny said. "Even though my father thought it was hideous. And there were always dozens of crows outside the windows on the telephone lines. That was all demolished though, after the party. But why would it turn into a...."

"A dump?" I asked.

"Yeah..." her voice drifted off. "If it's in the House of Coventry now, then...."

"Then my Realm is being changed," Archie said. "I currently can't maintain it from the outside. And clearly the guy in charge of it right now can't maintain it either, for a variety of reasons."

"Why would that die bring Stella to your destroyed childhood home?" Ellie asked. "When they didn't bring Nora anywhere and she's been touch-

216

ing those things since April?"

"Perhaps it's because Stella is the Jainkohilt-zaile," Penny answered. "Things work differently for her."

"But why your childhood home?" I asked, still confused.

"Because they're corpse-dice," Penny answered. "They seem to have brought you to the place where my family was killed."

"*Corpse-dice?!?!*" Nora squeaked. "What are those???"

"It's a common lejerdemani device," Penny explained. "Dice translates from Italian as 'says.' And dice is also playing dice in English, of course. It's a magical play on the word, really. You use corpse-dice by putting one into the mouth of a recently deceased person and then when you take it out the body will tell you why it died, how it died, who killed it, etc."

"So six dice means there were six…" Ellie stopped herself short.

"*Corpses*," Nora finished. Her face grew pale. "*Each of those things has been in a dead person's mouth?!?!?* Excuse me. I have to go to the bathroom and throw up right now."

"I'll follow you. I need to go wash my hands," I

said as I scrambled off the bed to join her.

"There weren't six corpses though," Penny said. "Only five."

And just then a black die popped out of the nightstand drawer and landed at my feet.

"*Don't touch it!!!*" my father screamed.

Duh, Dad.

Just. Duh.

"Oh, yeah! And there's a tiny robot in my drawer throwing these disgusting dead body dice onto the floor," Nora said while pointing at the nightstand.

Penny quickly stepped over to the drawer and took out a tiny robot, seemingly made from a mustard tin and spoons.

Archie gasped.

"Let me see that," he said as he hopped up onto the bed and reached for the robot, which then tried to nestle into his belly fluff.

Man, that stuff was so soft-looking.

Then Archie jumped down onto the floor and stared at the black die.

He gingerly picked it up from the floor while I winced, expecting him to instantaneously vanish.

But he didn't.

He was still standing there, holding a die and a

robot.

But me. Me?

I had a sudden, excruciating migraine.

"This must only work for Stella," he said as he offered the die to me.

My father—having noticed the floating black die—stepped in between me and the object in question.

"I have no idea what's happening right now, but I think we need to resolve that Pu issue before *anything* else happens today, okay?" he said.

Archie nodded in agreement and then put the black die back into the bag it had been living in while inside the drawer. And my headache instantly stopped.

Huh. Well, that explains why I've had horrific migraines since April.

"No one touches that die anymore," I said. "I think it's been giving me my headaches."

"What do you mean?" my father asked.

"When Archie was holding it my head exploded with pain."

"Wait, so every time Nora rolled those dice for her stupid game while she took a poo, you'd get migraines? Even though you were all the way in L.A.?" Ellie asked.

"I think so," I answered.

"Oh," Nora whispered. "My bad."

Several Minutes Later...

My father was still yelling about the dice, and my migraines, and why dice would cause migraines, and Archie, and essentially how screwed up everything was.

"He has angry management issues," I heard Morrow whisper to Ellie.

"His management issues aren't angry, Morrow. He has *anger* management issues," she whispered back.

CHAPTER TWELVE.

Later, In Penny's Grandfather's Study.

As Presented by Stella.

Penny and Eagle led my father, Archie, and me into her grandfather's study.

We left the three sisters behind in the kitchen. After they whined at Penny for several minutes to be allowed to participate in this releasing poo thing. Whatever this releasing poo thing was. Which I hoped wasn't what it sounded like.

The sisters weren't allowed to join us and were instead put in charge of preparing dinner. They didn't quite seem old enough to be making a whole dinner for six people and two furry things, but nevertheless, I hoped dinner would involve avocados.

The study seemed to be bigger than the cottage it was inside of. How did that work? No one else seemed concerned with that part of this situation, however. So we all sat down in big, old leather armchairs, while I looked around at the intimidating space.

I felt like I had just been sent to the principal's office in some antique boarding school where even the dust had an aura of grave significance.

"Look cat-god thing—I mean Archie, you know what you're supposed to do, right?" my father asked—the chair with Eagle in it, because he had no idea where Archie was actually sitting.

"Yes," Archie answered.

"He said yes," Penny said and then sighed.

"Good, good. And don't screw it up," my father muttered, still pointing at the wrong armchair.

What was he going on about???

And was it really such a good idea to treat a god with such obvious disrespect?

Couldn't Archie get really ticked off and permanently turn my father into a singing parrot or something? Shouldn't he be more scared of that kind of thing?

"Let's try to look at the bigger picture, Derek," Penny suggested. "Alright Stella, most of us need three things in order to practice basic lejerdemani magic: a signature metal power bracelet, a signature pigment, and a shadow creature. The bracelet captures and channels the force of the pigment, which is essentially a stream of universal energy that makes spells possible.

"A shadow creature isn't necessary for you to practice magic because you are the Godkiller, according to Archie. But also according to Archie, Sylvie still had a signature power bracelet and a pigment. So we'll start with calling on those in order to try and stabilize your powers before we release Pu."

"Isn't anybody going to explain to me what releasing poo means?" I asked.

"Later," my father huffed.

Wasn't 'later,' now? Wasn't this the moment when what was happening should be explained to me? Was I doomed to be perpetually in the dark? And was I really going to release poo all over this really expensive-looking Persian rug or something? Please god, no. Not that.

Penny had stood up and was unlocking a large black cabinet. She took out a fancy, carved wooden box that looked older than dirt. It had a hole in the top of it.

My father's back stiffened, and he glared at Eagle —still thinking it was Archie.

"Stella, push your sleeve up and away from your dominant hand," Penny explained. "And put your hand in this box."

Then she held the box out in front of me, expectantly.

"Is this one of those 'what's in the box?' games where it's cooked spaghetti and you tell me it's slimy earthworms?" I asked.

My father winced at me.

Penny smiled.

But I could see the pain behind her eyes.

At that moment I decided my comedy skilz were not going to be appreciated by this audience. So I obediently stuck my right hand into the box and felt a bracelet clamp around my wrist, sort of like a handcuff, and then I swiftly drew out my hand.

"*What the #*%$ kind of metal is that?!*" Eagle asked, jumping down from his seat and into my lap to examine it more closely.

"Huh," Penny reacted.

"What? What is it?" my father asked, unable to see the silvery-charcoal grey band on my wrist.

"I don't know what it is," Penny said. "I've never

seen it before."

"Oh, great!" my father moaned. "This just gets better and better."

"It's rhenium," Archie said. "The signature metal of the Jainkohiltzaile."

"Oh," Penny replied. "I see."

"Did the cat just say something? What did the cat say?" my father asked.

"He said it's rhenium, Derek, now let's move on," Penny said.

"It would have been nice if *someone* had told us the bracelet wasn't going to be one of the eight core lejerdemani metals, so when I saw it I didn't look like an idiot," Eagle murmured under his breath. But not really under his breath, as he pouted at Archie.

Then Penny went over to one of the bookcases and pulled down on a hidden latch. The bookcase rotated 180 degrees into the wall and was replaced by a card catalog with at least a hundred tiny, labeled drawers.

"Next, we will find your signature pigment in this catalog. Hold up your right hand and say '*indarra duzun deitu behar dut*,'" Penny instructed me.

I stared blankly at her.

"You're kidding, right? I can't say that. What language is that? Some magical abracadabra stuff?" I asked.

"It's Basque. One of the old languages of the lejerdemani. Not abracadabra stuff. Though that word comes from Greek and Latin, which we also use, but not as much. But anyway, say: '*indarra duzun deitu behar dut*.' This essentially means: 'I have the strength to call on you.'"

This time she had said it more slowly: Indian decent diet beehive dude.

That was it, right?

Nope. That wasn't it.

Penny still had to say it for me six more times before I managed to say it all out loud, properly— sort of.

"As a lejerdemani learns to cast spells, bands of his or her signature pigment appear on his or her dominant arm," Penny explained. "This spell will call your signature pigment to you, from one of these drawers, and it will fuse with the bracelet."

"Um," Archie tried to say something.

"So I'm gonna have tattoos!?!?!" I asked, slightly excited, and totally interrupting Archie.

My father groaned.

"Well, yes," Penny answered. "But you can hide them if you want to. I don't usually show mine."

She pushed up her right sleeve to reveal six blue bands on her arm.

"They go all the way up my arm, but I'd rather not to have to answer questions about them every day to the girls. They aren't allowed to practice magic, and they would just be too curious about these," she said. "My signature pigment is smalt, which is ground cobalt glass. That's why my bands are blue. Yours will probably be a different color. And the more you know about magic, the more powerful you are, the more bands you have. So as you get older, you'll get more bands."

"Um," Archie tried to say something, again.

"I don't need any stinking bands because I'm awesome just as I am," Eagle interjected. "You tattooed freaks, ppssshhhh."

"Ignore him," Penny said.

Alright. Okay. I could do this.

I was holding my right hand up to the cabinet of drawers.

I had my bracelet on.

I had said the 'Indian decent diet beehive dude' line.

But nothing was happening.

We all stood staring at the cabinet like idiots —well, except for Archie, who was looking somewhere else.

"Um," he started up once again.

If he had something to say, why didn't he just say it?

"What's supposed to happen again?" I asked.

"A drawer should open and a cloud of the pigment should come out of it and go into your bracelet," Penny said.

We stared at the cabinet even harder than before.

But no drawer was opening.

"Um, guys—it's not going to be in the drawers," Archie said as he pointed toward a fish tank full of black water.

A thin stream of black water had started floating up into the air out of the tank and toward me.

"*What is that?!?!*" I yelped as I backed away.

"What's going on?" my father asked as he stood up.

"It's okay, it's okay," Penny said, trying to calm us both. "Just hold out your wrist and let it go into the bracelet."

"No, really. Really? *Oh my—what is that???* That's sooo creepy-looking!!!" I jabbered.

The black ribbon of nightmares was almost next to me.

"It's just octopus ink," Archie said, totally calm. "That's usually the signature pigment of Jainko-hiltzailes. Just let it go into the bracelet. It will all be okay."

"Wait. *Octopus pee?!?* You want me to let a stream of octopus pee touch me???" I interrupted.

"*It's what?!?!*" my father demanded.

"This is a first for me, too," something from inside the black tank called out.

I assumed it was the octopus talking.

The. Octopus. Was. Talking.

Also creepy.

"It's not pee. It's ink. Two different things. Ink is like—mucus," Archie said.

"Blerghhhh," I gagged and tried not to throw up as the stream touched the bracelet and was sucked into it. "So it's octopus snot. *Soooo* much better than pee."

Then a black band appeared on my arm within an instant. And then another. And another. And another. Within ten seconds I had six bands, and more and more appeared.

I looked at Penny and Archie in panic.

"You're kidding me, right?" I asked them. "What's going on?"

Penny looked back at me, also clearly in panic.

"This is what usually happens to the Jainkohilt-zaile," Archie commented, still completely calm. "Their power is nearly immeasurable."

"I…" I began to voice my panic in what would most likely be a full-on screaming and sobbing fit.

But Penny slowly and subtly shook her head 'no.'

Her facial expression said—'don't freak out your father by freaking out.'

But I had black bands all the way up my arm. And I am sure they were under my sleeve. How far did they go? Could they go past your shoulder?

And then they started to appear on my other arm.

Eagle's mouth had already dropped open, and he began pointing at me like the circus freak I was.

"Alright, that went well," Penny said and sighed with fake satisfaction. "But man, I have to visit the restroom."

"*What are you talking about?!?!*" Eagle shouted. "That girl is covered in black stripes! She's a freaking zebra! Something is terribly wrong about this! What just happened?!?!"

"It's normal, it's normal," Archie said as he raised his paws up in the air, waving them back and forth like that would be a reassuring gesture.

"What's going on?!" my father asked, still standing.

Penny looked at my father and smiled.

Then she looked at me and smiled.

"Uh, yeah," I said and nodded, understanding her cue. "I kinda have to pee after all of that orange juice this morning."

"You guys are nuts. *Nuts*. We just came in here, and you both have to pee?" my father scoffed.

"Women, huh?" Penny said and laughed, as she coaxed me out of the study and toward the bathroom. "We'll be right back, Derek!"

"Wait, what's going on?" my father asked again as we left the room. "Do they really have to pee?"

"That girl is a freak!!! She needs to be locked in a cage for observation!!!" Eagle screamed after us.

"I'm telling you—it's really normal!" Archie insisted.

"Won't my Dad wonder why we are both in the bathroom at once, together?" I whispered to Penny as we headed down the hallway.

"Men don't pay attention to that stuff," she whispered back.

In the bathroom I quickly took off my sweatshirt to see where the stripes went.

They went everywhere.

Penny's eyes were wider than I'd ever seen anybody's eyes.

"*Holy crr-ud,*" she whispered.

I was a bit embarrassed to take off my pants in front of a complete stranger, but I was covered in octopus mucus bands, so I took them off. I needed to see it all.

"*They're everywhere,*" Penny confirmed.

And they were indeed everywhere. From my neck all the way down over my toes—which I discovered after I unceremoniously pulled my socks off.

"I've never seen anything like this," she said. "We can't tell your father."

Oh, great.

The solution to this amazing issue was—don't tell my father.

"But—is this bad? Is there something wrong with me???"

"Archie says it's normal," she replied, but I could see the confusion on her face and that just wasn't very comforting.

"Normal? This is normal?!" I pondered out loud pointing to my striped skin.

"How do you feel? Do you feel sick at all?" Penny asked.

"No, I don't feel sick. Other than the fact that my heart is racing because I instantly gained 700 tattoos!"

"It's okay. It will all be okay—like I said, there is a spell to hide them. And Archie said this is normal, so as long as you feel okay, we can move forward and release Pu."

Was she nuts???

I was ready to pass out.

Was this all really going the way it was supposed to go?

"Are you sure???" I pleaded. "This is insane! Look at me! I do look like a zebra! Are we sure this is normal just because Archie says so???"

"No, really—this is fine. Just fine," she said, nodding. "It's all okay, and fine."

Was she trying to convince me or herself?

I looked in the mirror.

Luckily the bands didn't cover my face so I didn't look like a complete freak—but I couldn't help staring at myself in shock.

No, no.

I was wrong.

I did indeed look like a complete freak.

"I see London, I see France, I see Stella's underpants!!!" Eagle sang through the crack in the door.

Penny rolled her eyes, and called out, "That's not necessary, Eagle!"

I put my clothes back on and we returned to the study where Penny set up a canvas on an easel and had me sit in front of it on a stool.

I was still shaking a little bit because of my sudden tattoo-ification, but I tried to hide it in front of my father.

"Don't worry. It's normal," Archie said to me, nodding.

If he said the word 'normal' one more time....

But I smiled at him just the same.

I was unable to reply to him without my voice cracking, as I could feel a lump in the back of my throat already. So I stuck with only the smile.

How can this possibly be normal?

Penny handed me a silver whistle and told me to blow into it. There was no sound. It was then I realized this woman was clearly insane.

"There's no sound..." I began.

"It's a *dog whistle*, you blockhead," Eagle stopped me mid-sentence. "That's why you can't hear it."

A tiny red, long-haired dachshund appeared in the canvas.

He was the size of my pinky finger.

I blinked several times.

He blinked back.

"Hey guys, whassup? Long time no-see—Penny, Eagle, Derek," he said. "Whassup, strange girl. Strange cat-god. How's it hanging?"

"Hey Hans, you fat-bellied fishmonger, you haven't been replaced yet, huh?" Eagle asked him.

"Not yet, not yet, you villainous jerk-weasel," Hans replied. "I see we have a new victim today in this strange girl. Nice to meet you, new victim. My name is Hans and I'll be drawing your shadow creature today."

"He's going to what?" I directed my question to Penny.

"He usually sketches the outline of your shadow creature and then you draw it out of the canvas with your bracelet and pigment," Penny explained. "But we aren't going to do that today, Hans. She doesn't have an itzal izaki. So you're just going to draw Pu in order to release him."

"No itzal izaki? Hmmm. Well, then I guess she must be the Jainkohiltzaile. Which is why she is so strange. No use in having Pu stuck up in this then. I'll get right to it," Hans said as he kicked at the canvas surface a little bit with his back legs.

I tried to gently reach for the tiny dog, but all I could feel was the surface of the canvas.

"He's *in* the canvas, you dimwit," Eagle said. "It's a portal to the shadow creature's realm. You can't actually touch him."

I nodded at him like I understood. I didn't.

"Brace yourself dudes and dudettes, this one is gonna be awesome!" Hans said.

Then he proceeded to bounce his way around the canvas, leaving behind a trail of tiny black pawprints that formed the outline in discussion.

"Baaa daaa baaaa daaa doo doo doo doo," he sang as he made his way around. "Da-da-da daaaa boo boo-bada bada-bada doo doo-da-da baaaaa...."

"Hans fancies himself as a scat singer," Eagle explained to me. "He sings this crud the whole time he sketches stuff."

I watched the tiny singing dachsund draw with his pawprints on the canvas, which was actually a portal to a different realm.

"Is this for real?" I asked Penny.

She nodded and said, "It's for real."

Had there been LSD in everyone's breakfast or something?

I looked to my father, but then remembered he couldn't see any of this.

He was lucky.

But he was still standing up, staring at us all,

waiting—with a deep scowl across his face.

After we listened to Hans scat for a good twenty minutes, he announced that he was done. But the sketch looked like a horrible mess of overlapping lines and curves and curlicues.

"We asked for Pu, Hans. Not a Rorschach ink blot," Eagle moaned.

"That's what I got from the strange girl. If you want, I'll try again. But I'm pretty sure I'll just get the same reading."

I stared at the canvas to try and see some shape in the lines.

And so did Penny.

"This *does* look like poo," I said. "Are we talking about actual poo? Like feces?"

"How can one person hold so much stupid in one brain?" Eagle asked—I am guessing in relation to my questions.

"Well, just because we can't see him doesn't mean he isn't there," Penny said and shrugged.

"What do you mean? Why can't you see him?" my father asked.

"*Are you joking?!?* With that thing as a sketch, we'll be lucky if he doesn't come out as a giant lizard monster thing with a tornado for a head!" Eagle insisted.

"It's not gonna be that, is it?!?" I asked.

"What? What is it?" my father asked. "What is it? What are you guys talking about? Didn't Hans just draw Pu as Pu???"

"Let's just try and draw him out before we freak out about what he might look like," Penny said. "Stella hold up your right hand over the canvas, and repeat what you said before: '*indarra duzun deitu behar dut.*'"

"Yeah—you're gonna have to give that to me again, a lot slower..." I replied.

I eventually managed to do as instructed.

Once I got the words out right, a shiver ran up my spine.

"I feel something," I told them.

"I don't see anything different on the canvas though," Penny answered, studying the squiggly lines as if they would jump out at her as something meaningful.

"I can't fight this anymore," I said.

But I didn't really say it.

Something else said it using my mouth, just like that time with the plastic container and the President of the Ernest Hemingway Fan Club.

"Oh, hey—Derek—you rotten piece of $%&* covered armadillo pus," I added.

I had just said that—to my father.

I had sworn—at my father.

I slapped my hands over my mouth. And shook my head 'no' as I stared at him with total and complete fear in my eyes.

"I've been so lonely, Derek. By your side. But always alone," I said from behind my hand. "Oh, Derek I hope you've missed me."

I had no control over what was coming out of my mouth.

That's it. I was dead.

Soon—I would be killed.

My father was staring at me like I had insulted his dead mother, but wasn't saying a word.

He was probably trying to figure out which of this study's books he could use to bludgeon me to death in the most painful manner.

"There's only one creature in existence who would say that stuff to me," my father said.

"Is it my fault that I feel things so deeply, baby? Why do you hate my emotions?" I asked him, blinking coyly.

There had definitely been LSD in my orange juice.

My father was *not* my baby.

My father was *not* anyone's baby.

Not ever. Not in the history of the whole world.

"There's only one *wretched* creature in existence that calls me 'baby' and that *wretched* creature is Puma," my father continued. "That's Puma, my shadow creature, talking out of my daughter's mouth. Explain that to me, Penny? Archie? *Someone?!?*"

"Well, it's progress, right?" Penny offered.

"Stella's a schizophrenic now!" my father shouted, as he turned to me. "Puma, how do we get you out of there? *What's going on here?!*"

"I'm still trying to concentrate and do my—that thing, guys. I promise. But I don't know what Puma's doing. He seems stuck," Archie said. "It seems to be unrelated to what I'm doing right now."

What was Archie doing right now?

He just seemed to just be sitting in his chair.

"Well, we put him in there, Derek. We can take him out," Penny said and then sighed. "I mean, he mostly put himself in there. So I think he's just being stubborn. Okay, Stella—focus on the canvas and say '*indarra duzun deitu behar dut.*'"

"It's not me talking, I swear. I'm losing my mind, here," I managed to stutter.

"We know. Just try and say those words again,"

she replied.

I smiled at her sheepishly.

For the moment all I could manage to do was keep my mouth shut. Whatever was in my head wanted to say a lot of stuff that would make me die of embarrassment. And then it was maniacally laughing in my head after I stopped it from saying those things out loud.

I turned back toward the canvas and closed my eyes.

"*Indarra duzun deitu behar dut,*" I managed to whisper.

Or something sort of like that.

The voice didn't respond this time.

Didn't interject.

Didn't call my father baby.

I opened my eyes and saw a tiny black and white cat appear on the canvas and run straight toward me.

"*Here I come Derek, you $%&*#%@!!!*" he screamed at the top of his lungs as he leapt out of the canvas onto my lap.

And then the cat stood tall, his back legs standing on my knees, with his front paws raised in the air clenched into little fists.

Triumphant—I think would be the best word to

describe the stance.

Out of the many things to notice, I would say that the tiny pair of pink little boy undies on its head was the most remarkable.

"Oh, great. You still have my shrunken underwear on your head," my father said to the cat.

"Why did my Dad have tiny pink underwear?" I asked.

"I never. I didn't," my father said and then sighed. "My mother stained them pink by accident in the laundry and then when I told her I was never going to wear pink underwear, Pu took them and started wearing them on his head. To taunt me. Endlessly."

"Oh, btw, I'm your Dad's itzal izaki, Puma. But you can call me Pu for short. Because I like to poo."

Then he erupted in laughter, at his own joke.

"Who doesn't enjoy a good poo?" Eagle said, sighing and smiling.

"Puma?" I asked. "Dad—did you name your shadow creature Puma?"

"It was the 80s..." he muttered. "We don't need to re-hash this all for her."

"I like hash and eggs," Pu added. "Can we have breakfast for dinner?"

"Wait—*so Pu was inside of me?*" I asked.

"Yes—sort of, well, in your soul," Penny replied. "We placed him there to block you from getting your lejerdemani powers. That's why your Dad didn't have access to his powers."

My father cleared his throat.

A horrid realization dawned on me.

"He's been in my head this whole time?!?!" I continued.

"Every breath, every poop, every fart, every burp, every dirty thought, every embarrassing moment, everything. Yes, I've been in your noggin for everything," Pu said while grinning at me, and reaching to touch my face in fake tenderness.

A look of horrified dismay dropped onto my face.

No.

No, please, no.

Let it not be true.

"I've even been torturing you by talking to you in your sleep lately, and writing your essays," Pu continued.

So that was him. Great. Well, at least that wasn't psychosis.

"You told me to die, you little pill," I said, grimacing.

"Oh, that one wasn't me," he said as he shook

his head. "I told you that before during that home-room essay thing. Some of those voices weren't me."

"Yeah—*right*," my father scoffed.

Pu shrugged.

"Wait—why didn't you tell me you were hearing voices, Stella?" my father asked.

"Um, because clearly I thought I was nuts," I answered.

"Well—okay—not to interrupt this very important conversation about the nature of insanity," Penny said as she tapped her fingers on a table. "I'd like to say that we solved the major issue for now, but we may have just made more."

"You think?!" my father asked her, his head tilted.

"Well, you can see Pu, which means your powers are back," she said. "That must count for something, right?"

"Yes, but I can *also* see that my daughter is covered in black bands like she is a walking bar-code," he said as he pointed to me. "Did you do that Puma?"

"Me? No. I'd love to take the credit, but the girl did that all on her own. She has an unbelievable level of magic. It's a miracle I managed to stay bonded to her for as long as I did. I was trying my best. But her soul was fighting with me every damn day. I mean, this girl is a freak. With a capital 'F.' She has a rhenium bracelet. I've never even seen one of those before! AND a signature pigment of octopus ink?!?! I mean, really? I didn't even know that was possible. Jainkohiltzaile or whatever, this girl isn't normal."

"I'm telling you guys, this is normal—completely normal," Archie announced, once again. "Totally normal."

"Yeah, *right*. This girl is either destined for greatness or she's going to bring on the apocalypse!" Pu responded.

I gulped.

Unfortunately, loud enough for the whole room to hear it.

"I told you guys—the Jainkohiltzaile, well, there's a different set of rules for them," Archie said.

"Yes—*that* helps, cat-god that I can now see. Thank you for your *great* wisdom!" my father said and then threw his arms up in the air.

"Let's adjourn this sarcasm-fest until after dinner," Penny said. "I'm too exhausted and hungry to listen to this anymore."

"Yes—*let's*," my father spat back as he stormed out of the study.

"Yes—*let's*," Pu repeated in a mocking tone and stormed out after him in a fake-angry walk with flailing arms.

"Don't do that!" my father yelled at him.

"Don't do that!" Pu yelled back at him.

I pursed my lips and tried not to laugh out loud.

A small black and white cat with pink underwear on his head whose sole purpose for existing seemingly was to annoy my father 24-7?

This should be interesting.

"What are we eating after dinner?" Eagle asked.

"We haven't even eaten dinner yet," Penny said.

"Exactly," he responded.

So we all shuffled out of the study while I wondered three things:

1) What was going to be served for dinner?

2) Could I go back to school covered in black bands? Or would that not be allowed?

And 3) Would I actually bring on the apocalypse?

————————————————

(Maple: Congratulations, friend. You've reached the end of *Daft and Deadly*, Maple's Fantastic Stories Book One.

Maple: If you liked this and want to know more about what happens to this odd cast of characters, please read Book Two *Distraught and Destructive*, and Book Three *Damaged and Diverting*, both now available as ebooks and paperbacks.

Maple: If you didn't like this, go back to the beginning and read it again because this is genius and you must not have been paying close enough attention to appreciate its profound beauty.

Maple: Sheesh.)

————————————————